Victory Garter

Maggie Sullivan Mystery #9

by
M. Ruth Myers

DEDICATION

This book is dedicated to members of my Facebook book club. Your love of all things Maggie, and your eagerness for another adventure in her world kept me going in this pandemic year.

ACKNOWLEDGMENT

Thanks to Stephen Grismer of the Dayton Police History Foundation, Inc. for helping me plot Mick Connelly's career path. We had fun.

ALSO BY THIS AUTHOR

Maggie Sullivan Mysteries

No Game for a Dame
Tough Cookie
Don't Dare a Dame
Shamus in a Skirt
Maximum Moxie
Dames Fight Harder
Uncivil Defense
Ration of Lies

Other Novels

The Whiskey Tide
A Touch of Magic

For ages 9-12:
The Great Leandro's Treasure

Victory Garter

CHAPTER ONE

I was in the city's most exclusive country club, seated across from the city's most exclusive madam. Her name was Mrs. Salmon and she'd asked me to lunch.

"You once told me my money was as good as anyone else's," she said when our rheumy-eyed waiter, who was eighty if he was a day, had shuffled out of earshot. "Does that still stand?"

"As good as anyone else's, and better than most." She'd helped me once after thugs who worked for a crime boss ran me off the road. I don't forget favors.

"Well, then, Maggie. I need the services of a private eye."

With her perfectly coiffed copper hair and understated makeup, Mrs. Salmon looked like all the other matrons in this bastion of money and breeding, except, perhaps, that her beige silk suit was cut a shade better and conveyed a shade better quality than the get-ups around us. She realigned her water goblet with the whiskey sour glass next to it, frowning at the starched white linen beneath them.

"I've heard just about everything in this job, so don't be shy," I encouraged as her silence lengthened.

"Shy." She chuckled. "Been a long time since I've been accused of that." Lifting her bouillon cup, she took a small sip and patted her lips with her napkin. "Here's the thing, Maggie. A girl who worked for me until a month ago or thereabouts got run over last week. Nice girl. Sweet. The cops have written it off as an accident. I don't think it was. I want you to look into it."

It was my turn to buy time while sorting my thoughts. I sipped some bouillon. My martini tasted better.

"You think someone murdered this girl?"

Mrs. Salmon nodded.

"Why?"

Two women stopped to exchange pleasantries with my hostess. Their looks at me conveyed not altogether approving curiosity. The little blue hat that topped my brown curls had cost a fortune by my standards. By theirs, it was what their husbands' secretaries might wear.

"Charlotte left me because she was going to get married," Mrs. Salmon continued as they moved on. "That's not unusual. A fair number of my girls leave to get married. It's what they all hope for, I think. Some, anyway. They know from the very beginning that if they want to leave, all they have to do is give enough notice and pay a fee for the upkeep and training they've had." She made a dismissive gesture.

"You don't want to know my business particulars. It's just that in this case…" She turned the stem of the sour glass between her fingers. She swallowed half an inch. "Charlotte was marrying into a very wealthy family. The young fellow she was engaged to was crazy about her, but I'd be surprised if his family felt the same way."

I let my gaze drift to the room around us and listened to the clink of china and the soft hum of conversation. A world untouched by the war still raging in Europe and the Pacific, it seemed.

"Are you saying you think she might have been murdered? That someone in his family killed her?"

"They wouldn't dirty their hands. They'd hire someone."

The very idea was fanciful. Mrs. Salmon didn't strike me as someone given to fancy, which made what she was suggesting even harder to swallow.

"Surely there would be easier ways of achieving the same thing. Buy her off, for one."

"And risk having her go right to Jack and tell him? He'd be guaranteed to dig in his heels. She was staying at his family's house, supposedly so they could all get better acquainted before the wedding. She called me right before she was killed. She was sobbing. Close to hysterical. She asked could she come to me, that she needed someplace she'd be safe. Ten minutes later, maybe fifteen, she was dead."

In that new context, sitting here amidst decorum and elegance and the other trappings of influence, her words were chilling.

Midway between the kitchen and our table, our waiter was inching toward us with our main course. As if she, too, wanted to sidestep the tension of what she'd just told me, Mrs. Salmon turned her head to watch his approach.

"By the time he gets here, my veal chop will have aged into beef," she predicted.

"I suppose Uncle Sam's taken all the younger waiters," I said.

"I suppose. I thought when Eisenhower and all those men landed at Normandy this stinking war might be ending soon, but that was nearly a year ago."

I didn't know how to answer, so I finished my martini. Her veal arrived still veal, and my minute steak bore traces of warmth, if only slight ones. It had been so long since I'd enjoyed any kind of steak that I was truthful when I pronounced it delicious.

"So, will you do it? Just have a look?" Mrs. Salmon resumed. "All I ask is that you find out what you can from the cops, Jack and the people in that house. If there's nothing to it, well, I'll eat crow. But I want to know."

Before I could answer, a woman stopped at the table to ask Mrs. Salmon if she was going to the bridge group on Saturday. When they'd chatted a moment and the woman moved on, I dabbed at my lips.

"Do you mind if I ask how you managed to become a member here?"

Mrs. Salmon chuckled. "I think your real question is whether they know how I come by my money." Her eyes danced. "A surprising number of the men who form the bedrock of this place – and approve new members – are customers, or have been. I'm discreet. I give to the right charities. To the women I'm a wealthy widow who made shrewd investments and is something of a benefactress to young women coming to town for musical training."

"Wow." I couldn't quite hold back a grin.

"So, returning to the matter at hand?"

"I'll take a few preliminary pokes. If that doesn't turn up anything I deem worth following, I'll let you know and that will be that. Agreed?"

"Seems fair enough. And you won't identify me as the one who hired you when you talk to the cops?"

"Not if you don't want me to."

"I don't. I haven't had any trouble with the police since the year I opened. But there hasn't been any trouble at my place that required them to deal with it, either. If I stick my head up, call attention to the kind of business I run, the chief of police is such a boy scout he'd probably feel compelled to investigate, maybe even close me down."

As much as I liked Chief Wurstner, I couldn't dispute it. He was fair and known for running a police force that was incorruptible, but he also went by the book.

"I'll need some particulars."

In the course of the meal, she gave them to me. The dead girl's name was Charlotte Littlefield. She'd been engaged to Jack Barrett, second son in a family that, if not among the wealthiest in the city, was well up there. The current head of the family, Simon Barrett, was more investor than active participant in the family business, according to Mrs. Salmon.

"His wife's in a wheelchair. She had polio, back before we entered the war, I think Jack said. There's an older son and his wife who live there, and Charlotte said there's a sister. In the beginning, when she was all starry eyed and sure everything would work out, she claimed they were nice to her."

"Had that changed?"

"I don't know. She'd called a couple of times after she moved out, eager to tell me things she'd been doing. Until that last time, there'd never been any hint." She gave her head the resigned shake of a woman who's seen too much of human nature. "I tried to talk her out of the engagement, Maggie. It's one thing if a girl who worked for me marries a nice, solid businessman. He can just say she was a singer, or was studying music before they married, and his acquaintances are perfectly satisfied. But marrying into a family like the Barretts, whose doings make the social columns and whose chums like any excuse to gossip about a newcomer, well... Charlotte's background was sure to come out, and I find it hard to believe Jack's family would grin and bear it."

As much as I agreed with her, I couldn't see them stooping to murder.

I thought for several minutes. She'd mentioned an older brother. Had he made some sort of play for the girl? Or had someone said something, done something, she'd misinterpreted?

"Are both brothers the age where they could be wearing uniforms?"

"I know what you're wondering, and yes."

She paused to return the nod of two men who were leaving. I wondered how many of the men who frequented this ritzy country club also patronized her establishment.

"You're wondering how the Barrett boys got out of the draft," Mrs. Salmon said bluntly. "The older one, I'm guessing, was deemed vital to the war effort. He has the day-to-day running of much of the family business, according to Jack. Some sort of industrial solvents, I think."

"What about Jack?"

"He has a bone disease. Makes them brittle and prone to breakage. One leg's already snapped a couple of times. He walks with a cane."

Our waiter took our plates away. As we awaited his return with coffee, I asked the question that throughout most of the meal had floated topmost in my mind.

"Does Jack believe what happened was anything besides an accident? Why are you the one asking me to nose around rather than him?"

"Jack, last time I talked to him, was still numb to the point of paralysis. When the police found her handbag, she'd listed him as the one to notify in case of an accident. They called him to identify the body, which he did." She turned her head to the side, her jaw tightening. "Apparently when she landed, it was full on her face. The only way he could really tell it was Charlotte was that she was wearing her Victory garter."

CHAPTER TWO

Back in my office I sat at my desk staring at the notes I'd made about the hit-skip death of Charlotte Littlefield. I'd turned thirty-one not quite two weeks ago, and I'd been doing private eye work for ten years now. I'd seen plenty of ugliness by so-called human beings toward other human beings in that time, but two things about Charlotte's death gnawed at me in a way that surprised me.

One was the force, and presumably speed, with which the car must have hit her to leave her features smashed beyond recognition. Had the driver been drunk? It wouldn't be the first time someone in the swanky neighborhood where it occurred came home from lunch soused. But the person at the wheel would have to be blind drunk to hit her so directly. Or, as Mrs. Salmon believed, it would have to be deliberate.

I made a note to check about skid marks.

Sadder than that, however, and more poignant, was what Mrs. Salmon had told me about the Victory garter the girl was wearing, the item which in the end identified her.

"The girls all wear the lapel pins too, like everyone else wears, when they go out," she'd explained. "Thing is, they don't go out a lot – just to get their hair done or shopping or if some of them go to a matinee. They don't go to teas or meetings like other young women their age. Their socializing's at the house. So one of them hatched the idea of getting special garters made up, with a flat rosette on the garter big enough for a Victory V-pin.

"It sounds kind of silly telling you, but they're proud of those garters. It makes them feel like they're showing their support of the war effort same as everyone else, and they get compliments from the men on them. I guess Charlotte had kept on wearing hers."

It had been her connection to the only family she had.

***

A stroll of half a dozen blocks from my office would allow me to do the preliminary work I always found prudent with a new case. It was a nice day for strolling. I went up St. Clair, then west on Third, and dropped down half a block to the front entrance of the *Dayton Daily News*.

The hit-skip that killed Charlotte had been recent enough for me to find what had been written about it in back copies at the front counter. There wasn't much. Because it occurred at almost mid-afternoon, it was too late that day for anything but a small item at the bottom of the front page in the late edition. It reported that a woman had been killed by an auto, along with the street and approximate time. Anyone who had seen it occur was urged to call the police.

A longer story on an inside page the following day gave Charlotte's name and age, along with a description of the stolen car thought to have been used. Again, anyone who might have seen anything connected to what was being termed an accident was urged to come forward.

The day after that, there was a bare bones obituary. Charlotte Littlefield, age twenty-two, died unexpectedly. It gave the date. It said services would be private. That was all the notice her passing merited, because she was a prostitute, not part of polite society.

Just for a minute I experienced some of the same indignation that had caused Mrs. Salmon to hire me. I shook it off and took half a dozen deep breaths. Then I went outside and crossed Ludlow so I could cut through the Arcade. I wasn't in the market for the fresh or cooked meats, baked goods or every other food under the sun sold from the stalls and carts beneath the Arcade's block-wide glass dome, but I was in the market for information I might get at a building called Market House which sat across from the Arcade on Main Street.

Market House was a narrow, pretty white building with row upon row of architectural ornamentation that brought to mind icing piped onto a cake. It housed the top brass of the police, the detective section and some specialized units. A municipal courtroom occupied the top floor.

It was the detectives that interested me as I went up the stairs. When I stuck my nose in the room that housed them, Lieutenant Freeze, the head of homicide, was at his desk. That might be good luck or bad luck. It all depended on his mood.

Freeze's dark hair was shot through with gray. He was thin, and not bad looking in a wadded-up-and-tossed-in-the-clothes-hamper kind of way. His eyes grew wary as they noted my approach.

"We're fresh out of stiffs. What do you want?"

"Your sunny disposition to brighten my day? To sell you dancing lessons?" I sat down in front of his desk. At the neighboring one, a chunky blond detective named Boike who was Freeze's prime assistant looked up from stacks of papers and nodded a greeting.

"Actually, you've already answered one of my questions, telling me you're not working on any homicides," I said.

"And I don't need you trying to turn something into one, so if that's what you're here for, go away."

"Just wondering about the odds a case the X-Squad's still looking at might be headed your way."

The X-Squad was a specially trained unit that investigated traffic accidents. Freeze groaned and reached for an Old Gold. We had a history, and it hadn't been the best. These days we occasionally managed a truce the size of a postage stamp, but we still got each other's goat.

"You're here to do exactly what I said – poke your nose in something and insist foul play was involved."

"The fact it happened a week ago and Traffic hasn't signed off on it yet suggests they might have some doubts."

"Yeah? Why don't you ask Mick Connelly? I hear he's in Traffic now." Freeze stood and motioned for his second-in-command to do the same. "If it's the hit-skip down where the millionaires nest, all I know is the car involved was stolen from a doctor at Miami Valley. And before you ask, he was in the Emergency Room working on a heart attack victim when the hit-skip happened. Nurses and another doc or two working right alongside him. According to a nurse who left work with him, he was mad as a wet hen when he got to the parking lot and his car wasn't where he'd left it. She had to give him a ride home."

I got to my feet, but the two detectives brushed past me with a haste that said they needed to get somewhere without delay.

"Hey!" I called after them. "Did the car turn up?"

"Yeah," Freeze said over his shoulder. "At the bottom of the river down by West Carrollton."

***

I spent the rest of the afternoon on routine work for ongoing clients. Those background checks and occasional bouts of surveillance paid the bills in between more substantial cases like the one Mrs. Salmon had brought me.

A little after five, I put on my hat, turned off the lights and headed over to pick up some mending I was having done. I'd scarcely gone three blocks when the bare-bones bus that carried Signal Corps girls from their boarding houses on Robert Drive to and from their work at one of the airfields east of town pulled to the curb and a swarm of them climbed off. As they approached me, I saw many of them were crying.

"What—?"

I didn't even get the question out before one of them blurted the answer.

"FDR's dead. The President's dead."

She started to sob again as two of her companions jerked her along, hissing not to blab.

For a good half minute, I stood staring after them, wondering if it was true. Then, quickening my pace, I made my way to a newsboy and bought an evening edition. There was nothing on the front page, where it surely would be, if only in a small, last-minute box. None of the newsies there or on other corners were calling "EXTRA! EXTRA!"

Apart from the Signal Corps girls, none of the other faces I passed showed anything out of the normal. The news must not have come over the radio either, I thought. Maybe the Army had gotten word first in case the Axis tried to exploit the loss of the man who had led America through the war from the terrible night of Pearl Harbor onward.

I headed for Finn's pub, which had a radio. After about an hour, there was a news bulletin. FDR had died two hours earlier. Harry Truman, a bland little man, had been sworn in as President.

I ordered another Guinness and as I sipped it, I wondered what this change at the helm would mean for the country. Then after a while, I took to wondering what a stolen car used in a fatal hit-skip turning up in the river meant regarding the death of Charlotte Littlefield.

CHAPTER THREE

I woke up in a world spinning with change. FDR, the president who'd pulled us out of the Depression and seen us through most of the world war we and our allies were fighting, was dead. Harry Truman, a man I didn't know beans about, had stepped into shoes several sizes too large for him to fill. To top it all off, according to the headlines, American troops were now within forty-five miles of Berlin.

"It doesn't seem right, him dying right when it looks like we're just about to win this war," said my godfather Seamus. A retired cop who had been my father's best friend and a regular presence in my childhood home, he sat with bony elbows propped on the kitchen table. The waves of his silver hair shook in disbelief as he read the morning paper.

Standing up, I removed half a slice of toast teetering between my teeth long enough to speak. "Yeah. I'm not so sure about Truman." I shrugged into my jacket.

"He'll do okay. They usually do."

Seamus lived in the finished attic of the tiny house

he'd helped me buy a year ago. He'd been puttering in the back yard when I tried to call him from Finn's the previous night. When I got home, we'd sat up late poring over the Extra edition which had come out by then.

He noticed my preparations to leave.

"You up to anything special today?"

I grinned. "Just visiting Mrs. Salmon's place."

His eyebrows raised.

***

It was Friday the thirteenth. Those of a superstitious bent would say that wasn't the best of days for plunging into a new case. Since I didn't worry about black cats or broken mirrors and similar hokum, it seemed just dandy to me.

With time to kill before I presented myself at Mrs. Salmon's, I tackled the next thing I wanted to do that day, mainly call Jack Barrett. I told him who I was, that I wasn't with the police, and that I was looking into Charlotte's death on behalf of a friend.

"I don't want to talk to you," he said in a dull voice. He hung up on me.

I called back.

"Please. I just want to get a picture of where she went that day, what she did, what she said. The littlest thing could help."

"With what? It was an accident."

"Was it?"

"The police said so."

"Actually, they haven't yet. After this much time, that means something's bothering them."

I wondered whether I should cross my fingers since that might or might not be true. Silence stretched to a noticeable length before he spoke again.

"Are you suggesting it was intentional? That's ridiculous."

"Then what's the harm in talking to me? It will put my client's mind at rest."

"It won't bring Charlotte back."

"She deserves better than to have the page flipped on her while life goes on. She deserves better than that pitiful little scrap of an obituary. Surely there was more to her life than that. More to *her* than that."

I heard a breath that wasn't quite a sigh.

"No one would want to hurt Charlotte, but if you think it would help... I have meetings for most of the day. Towards the end of it, I have an appointment downtown. I could meet you afterward. Five o'clock? For a drink somewhere?"

We agreed on a place and I hung up.

***

Mrs. Salmon's cathouse was a fine-looking big Victorian in a respectable neighborhood. The large front yard was impeccably kept, and two weeks into April it was a fairyland of yellow daffodils and assorted tulips. Opening the gate in the iron fence, I went up the walk.

A butler in striped trousers opened the door. He was younger and more slightly built than the one who'd answered the only other time I'd been here. Either he was the day man or a newer replacement.

"Mrs. Salmon would like a word with you in the kitchen before you go in," he informed me.

The day before, as we left the country club, she'd refused and then refused some more when I told her I wanted to talk to the girls that Charlotte had lived with. Finally, I'd convinced her that since they were the ones who'd known Charlotte best, and longest, they were the ones most likely to recall some passing remark she'd made, whether recently or years ago, about being at odds with someone. I wondered now if she intended to go back on our agreement.

"I decided they might be likely to open up if they were all together, so I've told them all to be in the music room," she said when I sat down across from her at the kitchen table. A newspaper was spread before her and a pair of small glasses perched on her nose. She was casually dressed in blouse and skirt. "You'll be able to talk to them one by one, but they'll feel safer being together," she said. "Like a flock. It's what they're used to."

She gave a playful smile. "They've had practice having private conversations in a roomful of people, so if any of them has something to spill without the others knowing, she will. But like I told you yesterday, they're skittish about the police, and because you're a detective, even private, you are tarnished in their eyes."

"It sounds like a smart approach," I said.

"Good. Let's get going, then." She sprang to her feet.

I'd never been in any part of Mrs. Salmon's house except the kitchen. As I followed her through a dining room and into a carpeted hallway, I was struck by the fact it looked like an ordinary, prosperous and well-appointed residence. No paintings of nudes graced the walls. There were no fringed or beaded curtains like the ones in the pulp detective stories I read.

The music room where the women who worked there were waiting more than deserved its name. In addition to the baby grand in one corner, I saw two flutes, three violin cases, and a harp almost as tall as I was. Tucked away next to a cigarette box on a low shelf was a harmonica. By night, the heavy blue velvet draperies at the windows would keep any trace of light from leaking out during blackouts, or at any other time. By day, they were drawn back, letting sunlight stream through sheer under-curtains.

"Help yourself." Mrs. Salmon indicated a table with a silver coffee urn and a platter of assorted muffins, then raised her voice. "This is Miss Sullivan, who I told you about."

A dozen women lounged around the room, some in simple dresses, two in slacks, one in a satin dressing gown belted tightly at the waist. Most were in their middle twenties to middle thirties, a couple younger. One I guessed might be around forty-five, with a sparkle that made her stand out.

None of the faces turned toward me were especially welcoming. Mrs. Salmon went around the room doing introductions. When she'd finished, I gave them a smile.

"It looks like this room lives up to its name. I take it some of you play the piano or fiddle or something?"

"We all do," one of them said, her arms crossed warily. "Except Lois and Jane. They both sing like angels. Not church choir good, I mean good enough to be singers at a supper club or in a stage show."

There were nods. One of the younger girls tucked her head and blushed.

"My hat's off to you. The woman who tried to teach me to play the concertina finally told my dad it would be a crime to keep taking his money."

That produced a few uncertain chuckles. I sat down

on the vacant piano bench, clasped my hands on my knees, and leaned forward.

"Okay. You all know I'm looking into what happened to Charlotte in case there's a chance, any chance at all, that it wasn't an accident."

There were indrawn breaths.

"In cases where a death isn't what it appears, the people who live with them or work with them are usually the ones who can help me the most. Jack's family won't be much use, she'd been with them such a short time. It's you who knew her; you she trusted. I'd like you to wrack your brains for anyone who might have had a grudge against her – even a small, silly thing. Maybe there was a customer who didn't think she'd treated him right."

I poured myself some coffee to give them time to think.

"Are you saying someone might have mown her down on purpose?" a voice asked.

"Most likely it was a drunk, or someone who sneezed or something and panicked when they saw what they'd done. Eliminating other possibilities will put some minds at rest though."

"Poor Jack," someone murmured.

"Yeah. He was so good to her."

They weren't talking to me, but to each other. I sat down again.

"The other thing that could help is any random

comment she might have made, either recently or a long time ago. One about something in her past. One that suggested an enemy or something she'd seen that she shouldn't have, maybe."

The faces turned toward me seemed a little less guarded now, although that might have been wishful thinking.

"In a few minutes I'll come around to talk to you one-by-one, so if there's something you don't want to say in front of everybody else, you'll get a chance then. First though, tell me what Charlotte was like. Help me get a sense of her."

"Nice," someone said.

"Yes, nice. That's it exactly," echoed a blond with a husky voice.

"Sweet, too," chimed in another.

In the ten minutes or so that followed, all I got was elaborations of those two words. She was happy, never made a fuss, always thought the best about people. If someone was down in the dumps, she tried to cheer them.

"I told her about our Victory garters and how Charlotte was wearing one, but I didn't show her one," said Mrs. Salmon. "Does anyone want to give her a look?"

The girl in the long satin dressing gown, who looked slightly bored, twitched it open and displayed a shapely leg. Two of the others stood and hiked their skirts. Each of the three wore a fancy garter encircling one thigh. The garters bore a two-inch rosette centered with a small, gold-colored metal V, a miniature of the lapel pins worn by women throughout the city to show support of American troops.

"I guess it helped her feel close to the rest of you," I said when I'd thanked them.

I stood and moved to talk to each woman individually. That was as unproductive as my talk with the group. Until I got to a girl named Audrey.

CHAPTER FOUR

Audrey was a cute little redhead with abundant curls and a permanent wash of color on her cheeks. At first, she said there wasn't anything she could add to what had already been said. Then her lashes flicked to see if anyone was listening and she dropped her voice.

"Okay, there might be one thing, only... Mrs. Salmon might not like it. That I went to see her."

"Went to see Charlotte?"

The barest of nods.

"Maybe she doesn't need to know. Why don't you just tell me?"

She brought to mind a little red bird deciding whether to stay or to take to the sky.

"We were close." Tears sprang to her eyes. "I mean really good friends. We met once after she went to live with Jack's family. We had a Coke together and she was feeling kind of bad that none of us, not even Mrs. Salmon, would be at her wedding. His family was planning it all, how it would be there in the house, just them and a dozen or so of their friends. Charlotte said it would be like she didn't have anybody at all. Of course she understood why, and didn't want to embarrass them, but still.

"Anyway, we got to kidding around. To cheer her up, you know? The next thing you know, we were hatching this plan that she'd pass me off as her cousin, tell the Barretts I was a singer and came through town from time to time. They'd still look down their noses at me, but I could come to the wedding. We knew Jack wouldn't give us away."

So far I hadn't heard anything that was useful. I tried not to let it show when the redhead glanced up to gauge my reaction.

"Then Charlotte got the idea that since we were going to tell this story about me traveling around to wherever I was booked to sing, she could say I was passing through and have me over for coffee. At the house. She said I could meet Jack's mother – she liked Jack's mother – but that there were lots of corners where we could talk and be by ourselves."

"Did you go?"

My interest had shot up a thousand percent. She nodded.

"Last week. Five days before she died. Mrs. Salmon teaches us how to dress and to buy good quality, so I wasn't an embarrassment. Charlotte took me upstairs to meet Jack's mother, because she's kind of an invalid and spends most of her time in bed. She was nice as could be. Then we went back downstairs, and... and..."

Audrey's hands balled into fists. "She was so ugly to Charlotte!"

"Who?"

"I don't know her name. Charlotte said afterward that the girl was best friends with one of them, Jack's sister or sister-in-law."

"What did she do?"

"We were sitting on two love seats in one corner of the hall where you come in – it's a really large house – when those two came tripping down the stairs. The nasty one stopped and gave us this look that could kill. 'Is one of those her?' she asked. 'Which one is Jack's...' Well, you can guess what word she used.

"The other one, I think she's Jack's sister, elbowed her in the ribs, but not in time. I think the sister was embarrassed, though. She tried to drag the mean one toward the door. But the mean one kept looking at us – at Charlotte. She kind of smirked, but it gave me goosebumps the way she did it. Her eyes were all slitty. She said... she said, 'You're going to pay for stealing Jack!'"

***

The two girls I talked to after Audrey didn't contribute anything useful. Mrs. Salmon, who had appeared to be deep in conversation with the girl in the satin robe, had kept track of how many interviews

I had conducted and knew the instant I finished. With a final comment that produced laughter, she moved away and set an unhurried course toward me.

"Well? Did anyone give you anything useful? You and Audrey had your heads together for a while."

"She's pretty upset. She and Charlotte were close, I take it?"

Mrs. Salmon nodded. "Like peas in a pod. Did everything they could together. You said yesterday you'd like to see her room. A girl who's been in training moved in the week after Charlotte left, so I don't know if it will tell you anything. Come on. I'll show you."

I followed her up the stairs to a hallway as tastefully decorated as the downstairs. By the light of two crystal ceiling fixtures, a maid polished wainscoting. Mrs. Salmon threw open one of the doors on the left.

The door once occupied by Charlotte Littlefield had striped wallpaper and sky blue accents. The tester bed was neatly made and heaped with pillows. There was a pretty little dressing table with perfume atomizers and a jewelry box, and in the corner a chaise longue. I wondered if the latter was for catching discarded clothes.

What was lacking were the small personal touches that might have told me something. A photograph, a book. The pictures on the walls set an erotic mood for customers already inclined in that direction. One was a finely framed reproduction of *September Morn*. Another depicted a damsel in gossamer attire reclining on a rock in a forest glen while a satyr dangled grapes above her mouth.

"When a girl sets up housekeeping, she chooses pictures from a closetful I keep," Mrs. Salmon said behind me. "These are the same ones Charlotte had, though."

I nodded.

"I don't suppose you recall any photographs she had?"

"From before she came here? She didn't have any. I can't recall anyone who's been with me through the years having one from before. Most of them are getting away from something they don't want to remember. She had one in a silver frame of her and Audrey, but she took that with her."

"Who got her personal effects? Have they released them yet?"

She was silent a minute.

"It never crossed my mind. I don't know if she was bringing her suitcase with her. Probably not, as upset as she sounded. If she left her things at the Barretts, I would guess they burned them or gave them to charity. Her purse... I don't know. You'd have to ask Jack."

Frustrated, I crossed my arms and paced a few steps. I'd seldom had so little to start with.

"Try and recall everything she said when she called you, even words here and there you remember. You said she told you she needed someplace safe. What else?"

The madam eased herself down on the chaise and gave a long exhalation. Her gaze was unfocused, staring into the distance as she thought.

"I think there was something about seeing something, or someone. I'm not sure, it was such a jumble. And something about a mouse... 'a little bitty mouse, not even a rat.' And how she wasn't going to be, or maybe wasn't, a mouse."

"You're sure it was a mouse she said she wasn't going to be? Not a rat."

She gave one hand a toss, then picked at a thread on the chaise. "I'm not sure about any of it, except that she mentioned a mouse and a rat."

***

My morning's efforts had gleaned me all of one half of one percent of a possibility. Audrey's story suggested there might be an irate former girlfriend lurking in Jack's background. But she didn't know the girl's name. She wasn't sure whether the family member with her was Jack's sister or his sister-in-law. I'd have to find out more when I met Jack Barrett that afternoon.

I thought about it as I ate my lunch on a bench on a grassy verge overlooking the Great Miami River, which wrapped around the city on three sides, embracing it like a lover. Every week a friend's mother sent me a loaf of fresh homemade bread that she tucked into a basket of fresh farm produce. In the eyes of the family that sent it, it was just a small Thank You for investing money I hadn't had to spare in a small business venture of theirs. To my way of thinking, I'd gotten the better part of the deal.

That morning I'd smeared butter on two slices of bread and tucked slabs of raw turnip between them. Now I enjoyed the resulting sandwich nearly as much as I did the breeze on my face and the squeals of a little girl flying a kite on the riverbank with an old man who was probably her grandpa. I'd seen the two of them and their kite there before accompanied by a little boy. Most likely the boy was now old enough for school. The chuckles and happy voices of the kite fliers provided a counterpoint to my thoughts about a death that looked less like an accident than it had when I'd agreed to have a look.

But what did I have to bolster that assessment?

Not the unpleasant scene which Audrey had witnessed, I admitted reluctantly. Yes, an unnamed girl had been vicious to Charlotte. Yes, her warning that Charlotte would pay could be construed as menacing. What it couldn't be seen as was an indisputable threat of bodily harm.

Audrey's description of the girl – mid-twenties, thin, blond – made me doubtful she would resort to actual violence. Still, a spoiled girl accustomed to getting her way, and with access to plenty of money, wasn't above hiring someone to commit an act she might later regret. Rich people had a tendency to construct whatever morality fitted their ends. Some years earlier, a new client's sister had tried to shoot me because she was drunk and mad at him, and upon seeing me with him, concluded I must be his girlfriend. A rich girl in a pique was more than capable of hiring someone to commit vehicular homicide.

CHAPTER FIVE

The cozy, old-money bar where I met Jack Barrett had walnut paneling on the walls and cut glass dishes with olives in one section and smoked almonds in the other on the tables. As I looked around, a man who would have stood just a few inches shy of six foot if his shoulders hadn't already started to curve, rose from a table in back and came toward me. He limped in spite of the cane he used.

"Miss Sullivan? Jack Barrett." He gestured me toward the table without enthusiasm.

"I suppose it's Mrs. Salmon who hired you," he said as he dropped the last inch into his chair. His gray eyes challenged mine. They bore the shadows of a man who wasn't sleeping.

"Yes." She'd told me that she'd called him, so it wasn't telling tales. "Since you didn't seem interested."

"What good would it do?" His voice, which had been controlled, finally cracked. "If the police start looking at it as a homicide, the papers will get wind of it and have a field day. They'll start to dig. They'll say what she did for a living. It's all I can do to protect her now, keep her name from being dragged through the mud."

He knocked back what was left of the whiskey on the rocks before him, then nodded to the nearby waitress that he'd have another.

"If someone did kill her deliberately, do you want that person to get away with it?" I asked softly.

"Of course not, but..."

"Which would you rather have, this all swept safely under the rug, or justice for Charlotte?"

I sipped the martini I'd ordered and ate an almond from the dish on the table.

"You think very poorly of me," said Jack.

"I think this has all been very painful for you. Taking another look at it will rub at the wound. I understand that."

He raked one hand through lank brown hair in anger and frustration.

"Yes. All right. I'll go over whatever you want; answer any questions I can."

He stared at the fresh glass before him but didn't touch it. I gave him a minute.

"What I'd like to know is everything that happened before Charlotte left. What might have caused her to take off when she did, but details from that whole day, really."

A noisy threesome, a man and two women, slid into

the table next to us. Jack's eyes didn't see them. He was looking backward in time.

"We work at home, ever since the war started. My father, brother and I. There's room, and we already had extra telephone lines, so when the need for space to house defense administration things arose, we offered our office suite downtown for the duration. That's to explain why we were all home in the middle of the day – the afternoon."

I nodded. "Go on."

"I worked through lunch without realizing I'd done so. When I came up for air, I felt bad that I hadn't been there for Charlotte. She'd gone out a few times for lunch with my sister and sister-in-law, but I knew she felt more at ease when I was there for lunch at the house.

"We liked seeing each other during the day, so I thought since I'd missed lunch I'd go up and see if she wanted to take a walk around the yard."

"How did you know she was upstairs?"

"How...? Oh. She wasn't in the living room, or the sitting room, so that was where she was likely to be. Unless she'd gone out, of course. So I went upstairs and was about to knock on her door, when I heard her on the phone. Crying. I could tell... I was sure she was talking to Mrs. Salmon – and that she was leaving.

"When I heard her hang up, I knocked and went

straight in. She was closing her suitcase. I reached for her, asked what was wrong, but she jerked away. She said...” Jack pinched the bridge of his nose. “I wouldn’t swear these were her exact words, but what I remember was, ‘I love you, but love’s not worth dying for.’ I called to her, begged her to stop, but she wouldn’t, and I couldn’t catch her. The—the elevator is at the back of the house, and takes longer, and I couldn’t catch up with her on the stairs. By the time I got down, she was already at the end of the driveway. In her red coat.”

He looked at me, his face a field of devastation.

“That’s the last time I saw her. Until the police asked me to identify her.”

His account concluded, he took a long drink of whiskey. His hand was shaking.

“How long have you had the problem with your leg?”

My change of subject pulled him away from the horror.

“Since birth. Why?”

“I was thinking it must be hard, not being able to run after the woman you love.”

“You’re the only one who’s realized that.” Taking an olive from the dish between us, he contemplated it, more for something to do than because he wanted it. “The common name for it is brittle bone disease. Three years ago, I stepped off the curb and my ankle snapped. Things like that. I'm not the robust specimen that attracts women, unless they're interested in my wallet. It's why I started going to Ida's place, I suppose."

"To Mrs. Salmon's."

"Yes."

"No girlfriends before Charlotte? Not one who might have been jealous?"

He gave a parody of a laugh. "As I said, I don't attract women."

It didn't square with what Audrey had told me.

"At Ida's, people were kind to me. Paid, yes, but genuinely kind, too, most of them. There I was just plain Jack. Look here, what you said about the police not issuing a final decision on this yet, do you really think that means someone could have killed Charlotte on purpose?"

"It's possible. Not necessarily the case." His account of the dead girl's final words to him made the size of that possibility larger than I'd believed when I sat down with him.

"Then I want to hire you. Tell Ida you're refunding her money. I'll pay whatever she was paying." He pulled a healthy sheaf of bills from his wallet.

"You're sure?"

"Yes."

"I'll have to see if she'll agree to it. If she does, then I'll need to talk to the other members of your family."

For the first time since his burst of assertiveness, he faltered. "I'm not sure that's possible."

"It's essential if you want me to do what you've asked." Leaning back, I folded my arms and grinned. "In fact, I'll do it one way or another, depending on which one of you is my client." Then something occurred to me. "They were aware of Charlotte's background, weren't they?"

"Of course they were. I'm a gimp, not a fool. I told them as soon as I'd asked her to marry me and she'd said yes. I told them if they weren't prepared to accept her, we would relocate."

"How did they react?"

"About how I expected. My sister and Tinker, my sister-in-law, threw tantrums. My mother was stunned, but she said if it was what I wanted, they should support me. The next day she broached the idea of Charlotte moving in with us until the wedding – so Charlotte and the family could get better acquainted, she said. I suspect she saw it as a chance to polish Charlotte a little. She found out Charlotte didn't need much polishing."

"And your father and brother?"

Irony twisted his mouth. It was gone in an instant.

"My brother was no stranger to Ida's. My father… whether he's ever gone there, I can't say, but I'm sure he knows men who do. I don't think he was pleased by my announcement, but he generally goes along with what Mother wants. Also, he's a pragmatist. There's no one else who can handle the job I do, since much of it has to do with land and enterprises my mother brought to the marriage."

"Nonetheless, I need to talk to them all."

I stood up, mostly to forestall any further argument, but also to move things along on what might finally yield some useful information. "You mentioned Charlotte closing her suitcase. Did she take it with her?"

"Yes." Gentleman to the core, he struggled to his feet with me.

"I need to see it. Her clothes, anything else she had in it."

"I..." He looked blank. "The police must have it. I never thought of asking for it. Or her purse."

"Call them. Today, if you can. Tell them you want to get it."

CHAPTER SIX

Mrs. Salmon had told me she was unreachable by phone after four in the afternoon. Maybe she was overseeing preparations for the evening ahead or maybe she was dressing. In any case, by the time I parted ways with Jack Barrett, it was going on six. Seamus was going to be at a meeting, so I headed for Finn's. If luck was with me, I might still be in time to get a bowl of the stew Rose made on Fridays and ladled out to customers who'd been around long enough to know about it and order some while it lasted.

I'd been going to Finn's since I wasn't quite eighteen. Until last year, when I bought my house, it had been the nearest thing I had to a home. I arrived in time for Rose's good home cooking. As usual, she was working the end of the bar farthest from the door, and her husband was working the front. She gave a merry smile at sight of me.

"Not here for your supper, are you?"

"That I am."

"Well, then, I'd better treat you right. It's been a while."

"Yeah, and I've missed it." Though I stopped for a pint a couple times a week, it had been at least a month since I'd come for stew.

Rose added the perfect topping of foam to a pint of Guinness that had been settling. She slid it to me with a wink.

"The man this was for needs to slow down anyway. Go on to a table and I'll bring the stew."

I settled myself, as I usually did, at a table for two against the back wall. Wiggling weary toes, I closed my eyes and let the familiar sounds of the pub flow around me. Even with many of the long time regulars gone to service with Uncle Sam and their places taken by strangers come to work in factories, the rhythm of conversation was much the same. It was pierced here and there by tones from places I couldn't identify, and softened in other spots by sounds of the south.

The stew that soon sat before me coated my tongue with its richness, and was so thick with bits of turnip and other vegetables that it left no room for regret of the lack of meat. A thick slab of wholemeal soda bread accompanied it. I was more than half finished when the sound of good-humored greetings drew my attention. Looking up I saw Mick Connelly coming in with his two adopted children. Instead of his police uniform, he wore a sweater and slacks. He noticed me and we exchanged nods.

Connelly had brick red hair and a hardness and

alertness of manner that came from growing up amid violence in Ireland. For years I'd resisted the force that drew us together, and his quietly persistent courtship. In a moment of weakness, we'd become lovers. Then, terrified of subjecting him to the kind of misery my mother had inflicted on my father with her cold, vicious silence and loveless indifference, I'd pulled back. I'd told him to find someone else, someone who could give him the home and family he wanted. When he did so, I realized I'd made the biggest mistake of my life.

At the bar, he and Rose had a good chat while she pulled him a Guinness. Once he had it in hand, he and the kids headed my direction. Brigid, the girl, was somewhere around nine now, and was drinking in the scene around her as if it were Rockefeller Center. The boy, a stolid little fellow, was maybe three.

"Hiya, Maggie. How're things?"

"Good. How about you?"

"Good."

His wife had been dead more than a year now, but there was awkwardness between us. His marriage had ended up being unhappy. It ended when Kathleen, pregnant by another man, stepped in front of a train.

"We've been painting the town red!" burst out Brigid. She sounded as thrilled at what was clearly a new phrase as by whatever they'd been doing.

Propping my chin on my fist I gave her my full

attention. "Have you? And what were you celebrating?"

"Dad got promoted to sergeant!"

"That does deserve red paint. What did you do?"

"Dad bought us all hamburgers, and he and Owen shared a milkshake, but I got one all of my own!"

I couldn't help laughing. Her excitement made her as cute as could be, despite the tight braids that emphasized her prominent ears. I held out my hand and Connelly shook it.

"Congratulations, Sergeant Connelly."

His chuckle warmed me more than any whiskey could. "Thanks."

"Well, I think you should keep celebrating, Miss Brigid. Why don't you and your brother go tell the lady behind the bar I said to give you each orangeade and popcorn if she can find some."

"Can we, Dad?"

"If you split an orangeade with your brother you can. We don't need any upset bellies from too many treats."

They scampered off.

"Okay if I sit then?" Connelly nodded at the chair across from me.

"Sure. It really is good news about the promotion, Mick. Will you still be in Traffic?"

He nodded, swallowing some stout.

"I don't know what I'd have done if the chief

hadn't moved me there after Kathleen died. No working nights like in other divisions, or not much of it anyway. He's a good man, Wurstner."

"Yeah, he is." I glanced at the bar, where Brigid was perched on a stool, talking avidly to Rose while the little boy looked up at them. "And those two kids look happy as can be."

His face softened as he ducked a look in their direction. "I think we're doing okay."

"Look, Mick, if what I'm about to ask you is something you don't want to answer, just say, but I'm looking at a hit-skip death that happened a week or so back, and I'd sure like to know why Traffic hasn't called it an accident yet. I was going to stop in on Monday—"

His chuckle overtook my words.

"I think I miss the old way, where you tried to worm information out of me."

"And succeeded half the time."

"Maybe more than half. It was fun, matching wits, remembering I needed to be on my toes."

"Yeah. It was fun."

Our eyes met. The silence between us lengthened. A silken thread which once had bound us to each other, and which I had thought severed forever, knotted and quivered.

Connelly cleared his throat. "I'll tell you the same thing about that hit-skip that you'd learn if you came over. According to the X-Squad there weren't any skid marks."

"The car involved made no attempt to stop?"

"Nope."

He checked on the kids. The boy, Owen, was starting to fuss, but was too big an armful for Brigid to lift safely onto a stool. She slid off hers and they started back toward us. Connelly, who had stretched his legs out and tipped back in his chair as he used to in days of old, sat up straight again.

"In fact, there were signs of acceleration. Just around the corner from where she was hit, one of the investigators found what looked mighty like tire marks – rubber burned off on the pavement where a car took off at top speed and its wheels spun."

Which could mean someone had lain in wait for Charlotte.

I pressed my hands together, pinching my lips.

"Awfully unreliable way to kill someone," I said, one eye on the fast approaching children.

"Could be that only injury or a good scare was the intent."

Before he'd finished, my head was shaking. "That's still unreliable. How would you know when Charlotte would happen along? How could you possibly orchestrate something like that?"

***

During the years I'd roomed in a house with eight or ten other girls, weekends often had a lot of time that needed filling. Now that I had a doll-sized bungalow of my own, spare hours seemed to take care of themselves. Even though Seamus saw to the lawn and cleaned his own room, that still left plenty of scrubbing and vacuuming. The chores gave my brain a rest from detective work, to which that contrary part of my anatomy often responded by kicking up an idea, sometimes from an angle I hadn't considered.

That weekend, while I was using a Brillo pad to attack the inside of the oven, I suddenly wondered whether the Barrett household, where Charlotte had been living, had any sort of routine or schedule that could have allowed someone to lie in wait for her.

No sooner had I hung my hat on the coatrack in the corner of my office Monday morning, than the chance to answer that question waved flirtatious fingers in my direction. My telephone rang.

"This is Helen Barrett," said a musical voice. "Jack's mother. He tells me it would help your investigation into the unfortunate death of his fiancée if you could speak to some of us. Eleven o'clock is generally one of my good times. Would that suit your schedule?"

CHAPTER SEVEN

The Barretts lived in the part of the city where money lived, south of downtown and the university. Although not officially in Oakwood, they were solidly in the area of cul-de-sacs and turreted houses on hills. Their place sat well back from the street on one of the smaller hills, but it lacked a turret. At the bottom of a long drive an iron gate stood open. To one side of the gate was a flat space large enough to park a car or two. In the morning sun, the white of the gravel driveway dazzled my eyes as I drove up.

A butler who looked more like a college professor greeted me politely. "Mrs. Barrett's secretary is waiting for you," he said. "She'll show you up."

As he finished speaking, a thirtyish woman with chestnut hair and a long, rectangular face bounded down the stairs like a friendly puppy. She hurried toward me with hand extended.

"Miss Sullivan? I'm Kaye Archer, Mrs. Barrett's secretary. She spends most of her time upstairs. She had polio, you see. Some days she feels up to using her wheelchair, but she tires very quickly. Are you a reporter? She doesn't usually see reporters."

"No."

She looked at me expectantly. I smiled. Accepting my lack of comment on why I was there, she led the way upstairs while I admired the surroundings. The house was a handsome place which despite its elegance managed not to be pretentious. It had the feel of a real home.

In the upstairs hall, instead of ancestral photos, a painting that was surely a Turner occupied pride of place on one side. The other side had a collection of woodland photographs, double matted and framed. In one, a teenage boy on a stream bank landed a fish. In another, a chubby little girl in rompers squatted to peer at a chipmunk. Most were nature scenes – trees with a shaft of sunlight setting them aglow; placid lakes, one with a doe and fawn coming down to drink.

"In here." Kaye Archer paused at a door.

The room we entered was large and sunny. Its walls were a creamy hue above the polished chair rail, and covered in wallpaper sprigged with tiny buds of green and yellow below. A cozy sitting room opened off the bedroom. What drew the eye, however, was a massive walnut four-poster, made up with a heavy green spread and piled with assorted pillows. Against the pillows a woman sat erect and fully dressed, with a crocheted afghan over her legs. At sight of us, she put aside a book and pair of reading glasses.

"Miss Sullivan? I'm Helen Barrett. Kaye drew up a chair for you so we could talk. May I offer you something? Coffee? Tea?"

She held out her hand. I could feel the fragile quality of the bones my fingers closed around.

Helen Barrett had been a beauty once, with her sky blue eyes and fine features. Illness had hollowed her cheeks and created moats around the blue eyes, but she was still a handsome woman. On second look, I wondered whether the planes of her face had been sharpened by illness, as I had assumed, or determination. Perhaps a bit of both.

I declined the refreshments, but took the offered chair. Helen Barrett wore a pleasant expression, but she was measuring me as thoroughly as I had her.

"Let us skip the social niceties and get to the point," she said. "You're looking into Charlotte's death because you believe it possible it wasn't an accident?"

"Yes."

"Jack seems to have come to that conclusion as well."

I was silent. Helen looked out one of the windows, her expression unreadable. She slid the bookmark she'd forgotten to put in her book back and forth between her fingers.

"What you're suggesting is monstrous. A deliberate..." She shook her head. "Frankly, it turns my stomach to even consider it. I don't like the thought of my son harboring any belief that it might be true, however. If this could put his mind at ease, I'll do whatever I can to help." She put the bookmark aside.

"What did you think of Charlotte?"

"Think of her?" She gave a surprised laugh. "When Jack first told me about her, her background and that he intended to marry her, I was upset, of course. No, not upset so much as... concerned.

Her mouth gave a twist. Her eyes met mine with soft directness.

"I wouldn't wish the months I spent in an iron lung on my worst enemy, but they gave me an abundance of time to contemplate what's important in life and what isn't. My initial reaction to Jack wasn't because I feared a scandal, if that's what you're thinking. It was because I didn't want to see my child hurt, either by her if she was a gold digger, or by the reaction of people we know, who would look down on her and snub her even if they didn't know the, um, details of her background."

"You tried to talk him out of the marriage?"

She sighed and turned her face away. In her line of vision now, if she saw it, was a copy of the doe and fawn approaching the lake which I'd seen in the hallway.

"Yes, initially. Then I met Charlotte. She was nothing like I imagined. There was nothing cheap about her. Oh, it was clear she hadn't come from a privileged background, but her manners were impeccable. She was somewhat naive, but she was bright and interested in things and very, very kind."

When she turned back to me, the flesh beneath her eyes was moist. "Once I got to know her, I realized she was the very sort of wife I'd choose for Jack."

A china clock on the table beside her bed ticked off passing seconds. I nodded at the picture of the doe and fawn.

"That picture of the two deer, there's one just like it in the hall outside."

"Yes." Her lips curved fondly. "It's a favorite of mine."

"Who's the photographer in the family?"

Helen Barrett cocked her head. "I was. Past tense now. Why?"

"Just curious."

"You're not at all what I expected you to be."

I smiled. "What about when Charlotte moved in here? How did the others take it?"

Using her hands as levers, she shifted herself, then readjusted the snowy afghan.

"Jack was delighted, of course. My husband and older son were polite, but too absorbed with work to pay attention, really. Kaye and Judith accepted it. I can't say how they felt one way or another."

"Judith is your daughter?"

"No, my husband's secretary. Arlene is our daughter and Tinker is our older son's wife. They live here too, Tinker and Noah."

I made quick notes, then moved toward the question in which I was most interested.

"While Charlotte was living here, did she slip into any sort of routine?"

Helen's brows drew together. "I'm not sure I know what you mean. We have dinner at the same time every night, or try to. Arlene and Tinker have their hair and nails done Thursday mornings, so they made an appointment for Charlotte as well. They all went for lunch and bridge at the club after."

"I was thinking more something Charlotte might have done on her own, like go to church, or walk in a park."

"I don't really know—"

The door flew open. A young woman with Helen's blue eyes and blond hair sprang across the room.

"Mother, have you taken leave of your senses, sitting there talking to a reporter? Where's Kaye? How did this woman get in? Why didn't you ring for Griggs to throw her out?"

"She's not a reporter." Helen was the very portrait of composure. "She's a private investigator. She's looking into Charlotte's death."

"Looking into – a private – she's a detective?" The girl's whole face reddened. Running back to the door, she flung it open. "Noah! Get in here!" she howled.

An instant later a blond man with thick shoulders burst in.

"What's wrong? What is it? Is—"

Kaye hurried in, practically crashing into his back. She stepped around him. "Helen, what's wrong?"

"Nothing."

A sturdy woman in nurse's attire pushed in next. "Mrs. Barrett?"

"I am perfectly fine." Helen enunciated each word. She smiled at the two women hovering in the background. "Nurse Wellington, Kaye, if you'd be so kind as to close the door when you leave. It appears I'm required to settle a family matter."

Her offspring had sense enough to wait until the door clicked before plunging in again. Arlene whirled to her brother.

"Noah, this woman is a detective! A-a private detective. She's here about Charlotte."

"Why?" The Barretts' older son seemed harried, as if other matters occupied his mind.

"Because it appears there's something suggesting it might not have been an accident. Because Jack wants it," his mother said calmly.

"She'll dig around and people will hear about it. People we know! Get her out of here. Drag her if you have to!"

"I may have lost the use of my legs, but this is still my house." Helen's silken voice had acquired an edge of steel. "I'll be the one to say who comes and goes."

Her thin hand raised for silence as both children started to speak. I realized she was trying to catch her breath. She turned to me.

"Miss Sullivan, I doubt we could have a productive conversation just now. I'll give you a call to discuss how I can be of further help."

CHAPTER EIGHT

My initial encounter with the Barrett clan had been too brief to form anything approaching accurate impressions. That applied to Helen most of all. The intrusion by her children had demonstrated how quickly she could transform from frail invalid to a woman accustomed to being obeyed. The frail part was true enough, though. I'd seen the array of pill bottles on her bedside table and seen the alarm in her nurse's face. I'd felt the lack of energy in her finely boned hand.

If she'd spent time in an iron lung, yet come out of it to lead anything approximating a normal life, she had determination. She was also one of the lucky ones. Every summer that I could remember, polio had been a lurking danger, but in the 1940s it had turned especially vicious. There'd been epidemic after epidemic. Some people who landed in iron lungs to keep them breathing remained there for years, maybe forever.

So, apart from the fact that Helen might exert more force of will than her limited mobility suggested, what had I learned about her? That she'd taken some very fine photographs, starting as far back as when her children were little. That she must have been willing to tramp through the woods to do so. That she spoke as if she'd genuinely liked Charlotte, maybe even been fond of her. Still, people could talk as if butter wouldn't melt in their mouths yet be thoroughly vicious.

Arlene Barrett, on the other hand, would happily have spit butter in my face. Her objection to my talking to her mother had verged on the hysterical. I wondered why.

I'd removed my nylons as soon as I returned to my office. The less they were worn, the less likely they were to spring a run. I padded to the window in my bare feet and stood looking down at the traffic on Patterson. Stories in the noon edition about the Allied advance made me think maybe the war would be ending soon. Maybe we'd be able to buy nylons again, and even silk stockings. Maybe we'd be able to buy toothpaste and all sorts of other things we'd taken for granted.

Maybe Heebs would even breeze into my office grinning, the way he used to do. A kid who slept in doorways and fed himself selling newspapers from the time he was eight or so, he'd won me over with his cheeky greetings and his pluck. I'd paid him to do small jobs when I could barely afford it, gotten him out a jam or two, and refused to help him lie about his age so he could enlist when he wasn't old enough. In the end, he'd found someone else to swear he was a year older than he was so he could sign up.

To my surprise, he'd started writing to me. Though censors saw to it that G.I.'s didn't say where they were, I had a feeling he was in Europe. His letters had come at least once a month, full of terrible spelling but guaranteed to make me smile. Now more than two months had passed since I had one.

The telephone ringing summoned me back to my desk. It was Helen Barrett. Skipping the scene in her room that morning, she got right to the point.

"As I mentioned, dinner is the one thing where we hold to a regular schedule, and everyone will be present this evening. If I asked you to join us, I'm afraid it wouldn't produce the results you need. However, if you'd care to join us for coffee at half-past seven, I believe I can guarantee at least some amount of cooperation."

***

I wore my dove gray suit, my good silk blouse and the strand of pearls my dad had given me for high school graduation. The others might be gussied up for dinner, but I wasn't headed there as a guest. I'd be there to work.

The gray-haired butler led me toward a living room the size of my whole house. Voices drifting through open pocket doors told me the family had already assembled. They were in a sitting area at one end of the room, nine people in all. Helen Barrett, in a rose silk dress and a gold necklace with a single diamond, ruled the room from a wheelchair in front of a white marble fireplace.

On sight of me, conversation halted. Arlene gave a whimper and sprang to her feet as the butler announced me.

"Miss Sullivan, Madam."

Smiling warmly, Helen extended her hand. "Do join us, Miss Sullivan, and forgive my not coming to greet you. Do you take anything in your coffee?"

Her secretary, clearly proud of her assigned task, couldn't quite overcome innate awkwardness as she filled a cup from a silver pot. On the opposite end of the coffee service a raven-haired woman sat with clenched fists, her gaze riveted on Kaye's every move.

"Just black, thanks," I said.

Kaye passed me the cup and swung her eyes to a vacant chair to indicate I should sit. Jack gave a welcoming nod that couldn't mask his discomfort.

"Perhaps it would help if I introduced everyone before I explain why you're here?"

Helen smiled again, a warning smile directed at the others in the room, I thought.

Simon Barrett, her husband, fit my image of an old-time sea captain. He was square of shoulder and not quite portly. His healthy head of white hair merged into a short, square beard.

Noah, the son who'd been dragged into the contretemps upstairs that morning, had brown hair and a martyred look that verged on irritation. Beside him on a love seat sat his wife, Tinker. She had an elfin quality, starting with her small build and sharply pointed features, and ending with an uncommonly short head of tousled red hair. She studied me with unvarnished interest.

Arlene, the daughter, hadn't warmed up to me any in the hours since she'd tried to have me evicted bodily from her mother's room. The turned under simplicity of her blond bob said she'd barely made it into her twenties. Boredom vied with annoyance for control of her expression. She sat with her arms crossed.

The other two present were Simon Barrett's secretary, Judith Todd, and his assistant, John McDowell. Judith, the dark-haired woman who'd looked annoyed when Kaye served me coffee, regarded me with chilly indifference. McDowell, the assistant, was bald on top and seemed distracted.

"Miss Sullivan is a private detective," Helen announced when introductions were over. "At Jack's request, she's looking into Charlotte's death. It seems there are aspects which suggest it could have been something other than an accident."

Noah, Tinker and Arlene all made objections.

"It's ludicrous!"

"Why bother us?"

"I don't—"

"Quiet!" Simon Barrett, stunned, turned to his wife. "Helen..."

"There wasn't time to tell you about it before, Simon. Miss Sullivan and I discussed it this morning. Upstairs. Until Arlene barged in, became hysterical and yelled for Noah."

Kaye Archer sat with her eyes fixed firmly on her hands.

Judith's hands had clenched again.

McDowell, the assistant, was gnawing his thumbnail so persistently he'd already drawn blood.

"I wasn't hysterical!" Arlene objected. "And even if what she says is true, it's no fault of ours."

"It's our responsibility. The girl was in our care," said her mother.

"'The girl?' 'In our care?' You make it sound as if she were some innocent—"

"Stop." Simon Barrett with arms crossed made his daughter's use of the identical gesture a feeble caricature. Despite the start of a belly, his broad frame and the way he carried himself made him an imposing figure.

Noah spoke with an icy calm that eluded his sister. "She's not only saying it wasn't an accident, she's saying it's one of the family!"

"I'm saying no such thing. I'm saying I want to get to the truth."

Simon turned his white head toward his younger son. "Have you considered that at all, Jack? That it could be one of the family?"

"Yes."

"And you'll let her dig?"

"Yes."

"Damn you!" Noah lurched to his feet and started from the room.

"Stop where you are, Mr. Barrett."

Whether it was my tone or the words themselves, Noah halted. He looked at me as though one of the chairs in the room had spoken. I smiled.

My next words were directed to Simon Barrett.

"If you have no objection, I'd like to at least establish where everyone was when Charlotte's accident occurred. I'll need to speak to each person separately."

I had to ensure they didn't compare notes. I held my breath. Noah's eyes flicked from his father to me.

Simon hesitated, then gave a curt nod. "Yes, all right. May, ah, Mr. McDowell be excused? He wasn't here that afternoon, and he lives at home. I'm sure his family would be glad to see him, his work keeps him here so late most days."

It took me only an instant to nod. If anything led me to think Simon Barrett or his assistant had something to hide, I could talk to McDowell later.

"Dad, I can't stay," protested Arlene. "Pammy is picking me up."

To head off a spat between father and daughter which wouldn't advance my cause, I spoke up. "Those who have something scheduled can go first. Will that work? Mrs. Barrett, do you feel up to staying here with the rest of them?"

She had the authority and intelligence to make sure they didn't cook up stories among themselves. After the briefest of hesitations she nodded, but to my surprise her husband spoke up.

"I'll remain here too in case Helen gets tired." Moving a straight-backed chair up beside her, he took her hand. She gave him a sweet smile. His secretary watched with the same intensity she'd aimed at Kaye's pouring of coffee. "You can use the small sitting room. It's just down there." Simon gestured.

"Thanks." I looked at Arlene. "Shall we?"

With a glare she flounced out ahead of me.

CHAPTER NINE

The sitting room was lovely. Comfortable chairs covered in worn velvet that had faded to tones of pale rose and tan jostled against tables stacked with magazines, a china cigarette box, a candy dish with cellophane wrapped Turkish delight, and the crossword puzzle someone was working. Terracotta tiles edged a fireplace empty of logs.

Arlene threw herself into a squishy armchair and crossed her legs. "Well?"

"You didn't like Charlotte," I observed.

Her mouth opened to object, then closed and opened again. "It wasn't that I disliked her. She was just… so different from us. Wrong. Wrong for Jack. Oh, God!" She wound her smooth blond hair around her hand. "I never wanted her to die! I just wanted her to-to go away. So maybe I wasn't as nice to her as I should have been. Maybe I said things I shouldn't have. I wish I hadn't, okay?"

"Fair enough." Now wasn't the time to explore exactly what she might have said or done that wasn't nice. Better to find out as much as I could. "Just tell me about the few hours before the accident and when it happened – what you remember, where you were. Then you can go with your friend."

Her response came so slowly I braced for her to refuse. Then she gave a one-shouldered shrug to let me know she was humoring me.

"I don't know. I tried to talk to her that morning, but she was in with my mother, trying to get on her good side as usual."

"Did she need to get on her good side?"

"No, but she was always trying to butter her up, reading to her, talking to her about things."

To me, her words sounded a good deal like jealousy. "Go on."

"That's all there is. I don't know where she went after that. Her room, I guess. I didn't see her again until lunch. She didn't say much, barely answered when Tinker and I tried to start a conversation."

"Who else was at lunch?"

"Kaye and Judith. Just the five of us. That's what it is usually. Sometimes Jack too. He came a lot more once Charlotte moved in."

"And then?"

Another shrug. "There's nothing much to tell. I came in here to look at a magazine. Then Tinker came in and we looked at some dresses. We talked about when we'd have coupons enough to go shopping. Jack must've gone upstairs, but the elevator's at the back, so I didn't see him then, just when he came down. Right before that Charlotte came running down with her suitcase."

"Did she say anything?"

"No. We both looked up, I think Tinker called something to her, asked what was wrong, but she didn't answer. A minute or so after that is when Jack ran past. Well, he can't really run with his cane, but you know. He looked upset and he stuck his head in and asked if we'd seen Charlotte. I said yes, she'd gone past and she had her suitcase. I said I thought she'd gone out.

"I don't know what happened after that. I think maybe he went to the side door to try and catch up with her or look or something. He came right back though. I heard him hit the wall with his cane the way he does when he's mad. Then the door to his office slammed. Then… I don't know how long it was… we heard sirens. Can I go now? Pammy doesn't like waiting. She may get fed up and leave."

I glanced over the notes I'd been taking.

"You'll call me if you think of anything else?" I handed her one of my cards.

"Sure. Of course."

"Thank you for cooperating."

She was gone before I even finished speaking.

***

No one else had indicated that they had plans that evening. It seemed smart to start with those less likely to be accessible if I didn't finish tonight. Simon Barrett's secretary as well as Noah Barrett probably fell in that category.

When I returned to the living room, Helen was nowhere to be seen. I wondered how precarious the state of her health was. Simon Barrett was reading through what looked like some kind of report. Since it hadn't been in evidence before, he must've sent someone to fetch it for him. During which time they could have hidden things he didn't wish seen, or done any number of other things for him, I realized. The others in the room sat in silence.

I invited Judith Todd, Barrett's secretary, in next. Although Judith wouldn't qualify as beautiful, she was definitely attractive. There was a tilt to her chin you didn't find in the average secretary even one at executive level like she was. Despite putting in what must have been a long day, not a strand of her ebony hair had escaped its Victory roll.

"How long have you worked for Mr. Barrett?" A bit of social chitchat might put her at ease, although Judith Todd seemed not the least apprehensive about talking to me.

"Ten years come August."

"Am I keeping you from going home, like I almost did Mr. McDowell?"

"Not at all. I have a room upstairs. As does Kaye."

"You must know the family quite well after ten years."

"Ah. Perhaps I should clarify. I moved in here when Simon moved his office here, at the start of the war. He sometimes works very late so it's helpful to have me on hand. But yes, the others did come to depend on me rather quickly, what with Helen unable to play any sort of meaningful role in the family."

Not many secretaries called their boss by his first name. I wondered what it indicated. I moved my questions along to the day Charlotte died. As I had expected, Judith had spent the morning working in the office area and had come out only at lunch time. My hope was that she might shed some light on what had occurred in the course of that meal.

"I understand you had lunch with the others that day. With Charlotte, Tinker and Arlene?"

"Yes, Kaye and I usually join them. It gives me a break. I can sit and relax and listen to Tinker and Arlene chatter."

"And Charlotte?"

"I… Sorry. I don't understand the question you're asking."

"Charlotte, did she chatter too?"

"Ah. I wouldn't say she chattered, but she did attempt to join in. She was always eager to fit in. Eager for everything, really, poor girl." She hesitated.

"Now that you ask though, she wasn't as, well, animated that day. In fact, she seemed somewhat preoccupied."

"Any idea why?"

"I'm afraid not. I had very little contact with her really."

She had returned to her office immediately after lunch and hadn't been aware of anything that happened afterwards until Griggs the butler knocked on the door and told them there'd been an accident.

Since Noah Barrett was the most out-of-sorts of the lot, apart from his sister, I took him next. He stalked ahead of me without a word. In the sitting room he helped himself to a cigarette from the china box. When he'd gotten it going, he dropped into a high-backed chair and stared at me with open smugness.

"I wasn't here when the accident happened. I was downtown filling in for Dad at a civic luncheon. Anything else you want to know?"

"The name of the civic group would be nice."

It seemed to catch him off guard. He flicked the powdery residue from his cigarette in the general direction of an ashtray. With a glare, he told me. I wrote it down. We stared at one another. When I saw that wasn't going to work, I probed. "How would you describe Charlotte?"

"I wouldn't. The only time I had anything to do with her was at dinner. Mother's very keen on dinner together. Even the old man knuckles under."

Noah Barrett had too good an opinion of himself. It was tempting to grill him as hard as I could, but it was growing late. Knowing that what gave me satisfaction wouldn't necessarily gain me any information, I proceeded in a bare bones fashion.

"All right, then, based in what you saw of her at dinner was there anything different about her manner in the few days before her death? Was she happier? Quieter? Worried?"

He admired his cigarette. "Couldn't say. She was one of those moody types. Ask Jack, he's the expert on women."

Did I detect brotherly jealousy? "Meaning what?"

"Nothing. Just that he's the sort that women confide in. They like him, in spite of his being a gimp. Why he had to bring home a girl like that and embarrass us all when there were at least a few girls in our set who would have married him—"

He broke off, clamping his mouth shut.

"Everyone else in your family claims to have liked Charlotte, or at least been neutral about her."

"Well, they're lying." Jack stood up. "Are we done here?"

There was nothing to be gained by detaining him. I returned to the living room while he stalked off toward the rear of the house.

Tinker showed nothing of her husband's hostility. When we got to the sitting room she looked around as if half expecting to see him, then settled onto one of the love seats with her legs tucked under her.

"Okay, from what you said about why you're here, this is going to be like the police. They asked how I got along with Charlotte and where I'd been and what everyone was doing on her last day here. Is that what you want to know?"

"More or less."

She fiddled with a gold bangle bracelet, her expression wary. "I didn't like her," she said bluntly.

If nothing else it was refreshing.

"Any particular reason?" I asked.

She picked at her bracelet. Her eyes never left mine. "Well, what she'd been of course. Someone was bound to find out. And-and her cheap red raincoat." She swung her legs the opposite way and tucked them under her. "Okay, it wasn't really cheap I guess, and I know we have to take what we can get in the stores. But she stuck out and made us stick out. I know it's not nice to be snobbish, but Jack should have thought of the rest of us. So there. I suppose you think I'm rude, but I'm being honest."

Her account of what happened at lunch that last day was the same as I'd already heard. Something was bothering her, though. I couldn't put my finger on what. I decided to throw a dart and see if it hit anything.

"I guess the way she caught your husband's eye was something else you held against her."

She snorted bitterly. "Is that some kind of joke? Noah doesn't notice anything. All he does is work. I could trade places with a chimpanzee and he wouldn't see any difference, let alone care."

I'd hit something, but I wasn't sure what and now wasn't the time to poke at the wound. I walked with her back to the living room, the size of which was magnified now by the sparseness of its occupants.

Simon Barrett looked up from what appeared to be a different report. Kaye sat with her cheek propped on her hand, attempting to stay awake. Noah had rejoined them. He sat with legs stretched before him, glaring at the pages of a book.

"It's late," I said. "With your permission, I'll come back tomorrow to talk to Miss Archer and a few members of your staff – the butler, the housekeeper – and maybe ask a few more questions that occur to me overnight."

"You're welcome to come and go as often as you like." Simon got to his feet. His eyes narrowed at Noah, and at Tinker, who had gone to sit on the arm of her husband's chair. "I expect you to cooperate. Your mother wants this. I want this. Tell your sister."

I thanked them and said goodnight.

My first lungful of outside air didn't come a minute too soon for my taste. The currents I'd sensed in the Barrett home had tangled around me like ropes. I opened the door to my DeSoto, then noticed the rear tire. As I bent for a closer look, suspicion gave way to cold fury.

Of all the things that were rationed, tires were the hardest to come by. Impossible, really. While I was inside asking questions, one of mine had been neatly and deliberately slashed.

CHAPTER TEN

Twenty minutes after I turned on my office lights the next morning, I found myself in an argument with the Barretts' chauffeur. He stood before my desk as if an immovable object. I was good at moving things.

"You could have saved yourself a trip downtown, Mr. Hays. I told you on the phone I'm perfectly capable of getting where I need to go without my car. I certainly don't need you picking me up when I'm not ready to go anywhere."

"But—"

I held up a hand. I'd been plenty steamed the night before when I walked back into the Barrett house and announced that I needed to call a cab because one of my tires had been slashed. Simon Barrett had given every appearance of being outraged too. He'd insisted on having Hays drive me home in the family car. I'd given in rather than wait for a taxi. But when Hays had called my office as I was hanging up my hat this morning, my anger from the previous evening returned full force. Now the unfortunate man stood before me.

"Furthermore, Mr. Hays, I refuse to have anyone pulling strings to get me a tire. Please take it off and use my spare to replace the tire that was damaged."

Hays was, by my guess, at least sixty. He squared his shoulders.

"I won't do that, Miss. Your spare's not safe. Accelerate a bit or brake too fast and you'll slide into a telephone pole. Mr. Barrett didn't pull strings. He's not that sort. He said take a tire from one of the cars they drive, but neither would fit yours, so I did some trading. The spare from the family car to someone who needed that size, the tire from that car to somebody who had one to fit yours."

I sighed. Maybe he was telling the truth, maybe not. I needed a drivable car.

"All right, then, and thanks. But I'll get out to see the Barretts when I'm ready. I've got other things I need to do here."

A moment's hesitation and he nodded. After he left, I felt bad about the hard time I'd given him. Then I went back to considering the event which had brought him here.

By slashing my tire, someone had sent a powerful message: They didn't want me looking into Charlotte Littlefield's death. The question was: Why? Was it because they'd had something to do with it, or because they didn't want me causing ripples in their peaceful, privileged existence? All families had dirty linen, but those with money fought hard to keep theirs from being aired. Or maybe, as Arlene had suggested, they didn't want notoriety; didn't want to be the subject of gossip at the country club.

Since I didn't have any answers there, I wound a sheet of paper into the Remington to begin typing up my notes from the previous night to see what those might suggest. I was still at it an hour later when Jack Barrett called.

"I got the suitcase," he said. "And her purse. I took them to Ida's. I couldn't..."

"Sure."

"Ida said you could stop by this morning if it fits your schedule."

***

It had never occurred to me a madam might have an office, but Ida Salmon was a businesswoman to the core. The office was a small room at the rear of the upstairs hallway. With the door open, she could keep an eye on all the comings and goings in the bedrooms as well as on the back staircase.

Right now, the door was closed. She gestured to a scraped and dented suitcase on a long table shoved against one wall.

"It looked practically new when she left. Now the frame's sprung and, well, you can see for yourself. I guess they tied it closed down at the police station."

I was too busy looking at it to answer. There were

dark stains on the suitcase which I knew to be blood. One corner had been crushed by impact. When I undid the twine wrapped around it, the lid popped askew.

"Want a brandy?" asked Mrs. Salmon.

"No, thanks."

Pouring one for herself, she came to my side. I lifted the lid.

Clothes were stuffed in haphazardly, whether from Charlotte's speed in departing, or being tossed through the air, or having been gone through by the police. Tucked in between them was a snapshot in a silver frame. It was the one Mrs. Salmon had mentioned, of Charlotte and Audrey. *Friends to the end,* I thought.

"That would mean the world to Audrey. Having that," Mrs. Salmon said.

I nodded. "Go ahead."

An object at the bottom of the suitcase caught my eye. I lifted out a fold-up Kodak camera, the kind where the front dropped down like a drawbridge and the camera bellows unfolded on it. It was similar to the one I owned, only newer and nicer.

"Nobody mentioned Charlotte being interested in photography," I said.

"I never knew she was." Mrs. Salmon wore a faint frown. "I never saw that before."

"Jack's mother is a keen photographer, or was, in her day."

"Maybe Charlotte caught the bug from her, then."

"Maybe."

I was holding the camera up, looking at the film counter. Eleven shots used on a twelve exposure roll. I advanced the film, clicked a throwaway shot on the last frame, and advanced it some more until the tail of the film disappeared into the metal cannister. I opened the back of the camera and removed the film.

"Okay if I get this developed? See what Charlotte was taking pictures of?"

It was a long shot, but something on the film might hold a clue to what had caused her to flee for her life.

CHAPTER ELEVEN

When I left Mrs. Salmon, I took a bus back downtown. A few years ago, I could have dropped off the film to a photographer pal who worked at the *Daily News*. He would have developed it after hours and made me prints. Now he was overseas snapping pictures for the Army. His wife had taken his job at the paper, but the old lech in charge of the photo department watched her like a hawk. I couldn't ask her to risk a chewing out – or a pass if she worked after hours – for me.

Instead, I dropped off the film at a place with a respectable business in front and a room that took girlie pictures in back. For triple the usual price they promised to have prints from the film in Charlotte's camera by the following day. From there I caught a bus down Patterson. It gave me a chance to see the approach to the Barrett house and the stretch of road where the hit-skip occurred from a different perspective than I got from a car.

My sightseeing didn't tell me anything. I got off the bus a few blocks early and walked to my destination.

A car was parked in the small space at the foot of the driveway. I wondered why it was there when there was ample parking up above.

The butler sent word up to Mrs. Barrett that I wanted to see her. He was turning to go back to whatever butlers do when they're not answering doors when I delayed him.

"Mr. Griggs. There's a question I expect you can answer for me while I'm waiting."

"I will if I can."

Cautious man, Griggs, and diplomatic, since 'can' could be interpreted as able or willing.

"Can you think of any former employees who might feel they weren't treated fairly here? Anyone who might feel resentment toward this family?"

He scarcely paused to consider it. "I believe anyone who has worked for the family would say they were treated fairly. A young woman who worked in the kitchen gave notice because she could earn more in a defense plant. A man who did odd jobs for us was asked to leave after several items went missing, but where's the unfairness in that?"

People whose change in circumstances was entirely their own doing often didn't see it that way, though. They nursed grudges.

"When was that?"

"Oh, well before the young woman who left. Four years ago, at least."

"I'd like both names, and any contact information you have for them, please. It's unlikely either had anything to do with Miss Littlefield's accident, but it never hurts to check."

"I'm afraid I don't recall their names. I'll ask Mrs. Randall. As housekeeper, she's the one who keeps track of that type of thing."

Kaye Archer came hurrying down the stairs.

"Was there anything else, Miss?"

"No, thank you, Griggs."

He went his way, and I turned to Kaye.

"I'm afraid Helen's still resting. Last evening was a bit rough on her. Can I help you with anything?"

"As a matter of fact, you're one of the people I wanted to talk to this morning. Do you have time now?"

"It's the perfect time. Will here do?" She gestured toward the sitting room I'd used last night.

As we settled into comfortable chairs, I felt a momentary sense that perhaps I'd nodded off and it was still the previous evening. Shaking off such thoughts, I asked the secretary how long she'd worked for Helen.

"Eight years. Well, eight and a half, really. A year or so longer than Judith." She smiled uncertainly. It emphasized her slight overbite. "I was Helen's secretary before she became ill and I stuck around. They – the family – thought it would reassure her that she was expected to recover and lead a busy life like she had before." Her long face showed momentary sadness. Producing a lace-trimmed hanky from her pocket she dabbed at her nose.

"Of course, it isn't busy in the same way, but there's just as much correspondence to deal with, maybe more. I think she likes the talking about what she wants me to do and my reporting. It fills up part of her day. When I've finished what I need to do for her, I try to make myself useful to the rest of the family. Jack doesn't have a secretary, so I'm glad to do whatever typing and dictation that he needs."

I'd been sifting through other bits of information as I listened. "You've worked for the Barretts longer than Judith? I'd somehow gotten the impression it was the other way around."

She gave a tittering laugh and raised a hand to smother it as if embarrassed.

"She worked at the Barrett company for some time before she started working for Mr. Barrett himself. The secretary he'd had for ages began having eye problems and decided to retire. Judith took her place. Oh, dear. Am I chattering? I tend to do that."

The differing versions of how long Judith had worked for Simon Barrett made me wonder if there was some sort of seniority tussle between the two secretaries. When I asked Kaye what she thought of Charlotte her answer surprised me.

"Well, I thought her rather splendid, actually. I suppose it's because Helen was fond of the girl." Her brows knitted in thought. "No, that's not entirely the reason. I would have liked her anyway because she was kind. I think she may have annoyed some of the family because she spent as much time as she did with Helen. She read to her almost every day. I know Helen enjoyed it. She's a terribly good sport – Helen, I mean – but I'm sure she gets tired of seeing so much of me and Nurse Wellington and not a lot of anyone else.

"I liked her because she was kind to Jack too. Jack deserves that, someone who cares for him for the person he is rather than because of his family name or money." She bit her lip, self-conscious. I wondered if she had a bit of a crush.

I asked her to go through everything she could remember about the day Charlotte died. It didn't yield anything new. After lunch with the others, she gathered up some letters she'd typed that morning and taken them to Helen for her signature. They had discussed how to handle the latest request for a donation to a charity group that came begging almost every month.

"We didn't hear Charlotte's phone call or anything else, really, until Griggs ran in to tell us there'd been—"

"Excuse me." Nurse Wellington stopped in the

doorway. "Mrs. Barrett is awake now if you'd like to come up. Mrs. Price is with her so she said I should have my lunch break now."

***

"I do apologize for running out on you last night." Helen looked pale today. She was casually dressed in a sweater and slacks. Her hair hung in a loose braid at the back of her neck. "I don't even know what to say about the damage to your car. I trust Simon found a way to remedy the situation?"

"He did, thank you."

"This is my dear friend Lola Price. We have no secrets from each other." They exchanged a smile that verged on wicked. "I've told her about what's happening as best I'm able, so you may speak freely in front of her."

Lola Price was small and dark haired and dressed in expensive clothes that showed traces of wear. She had the ways of the upper class about her, but her nod was friendly.

"Helen tells me you're a private detective. Do you have a business card? I should love to see what one for a detective looks like."

The request amused me, but I was glad to pass her one. Maybe she needed help with something, or knew someone who did. It was how I got much of my business, these connections to someone who had used my services. After studying it, to my surprise, she handed it back to me. Even more to my surprise, there was something under it.

"Are you sure you don't want to keep it? I don't exactly have a shortage of them."

"No thank you. My curiosity is satisfied. It must be very interesting work."

"At times." Before I returned the card to my pocket, I was able to glimpse what looked it might be Lola's calling card under mine. But why the subterfuge? "Most of the time it's duller than you can imagine."

Both women chuckled. I asked Helen what I hadn't had a chance to the previous day, what she remembered about the hours just before Charlotte's death. As I suspected, she'd been upstairs and didn't have much to add. Charlotte spent some time with her that morning, reading to her, which they both enjoyed.

"That was the last time I saw her. The last I heard of her." Helen's voice was sad. And tired. She hadn't heard a peep from Charlotte after lunch, including the phone call. "I usually nap while they're all at lunch, and did that day. Then Kaye brought some letters up for me to sign and we discussed things – I can't remember what. That's what we were doing when Griggs and Nurse Wellington came in and we learned there'd been an accident."

The woman wasn't well. I didn't want to tax her

further, but one last thing felt too important not to ask.

"There was a camera in Charlotte's belongings..."

"Yes. I gave it to her. I got it for Tinker last year, but she told me she didn't want it – Tinker's very direct. Charlotte was having fun with it, I think. She'd get her prints back and bring them in and I'd tell her what she'd done well and what she could improve. She had a dreadful tendency to underexpose."

Helen had begun to lean back on her pillows. I thanked her and murmured pleasantries to Lola.

"It was so nice to meet a real-life detective." She held out her hand. "I wish you the best with your inquiries."

Her eyes sought mine. She was trying to tell me something, or impress something on me. Whatever she'd slipped me when she returned my business card was burning a hole in my pocket.

CHAPTER TWELVE

"Are Helen and Lola really the pals they claim to be?" I asked Kaye when we reached the hallway.

"Oh, absolutely. They go back a long way. Mrs. Price is Arlene's godmother, possibly for Noah and Jack as well. She never missed a day visiting Helen the whole time she was in the hospital."

She gave a tentative smile. "We were interrupted earlier, when Nurse Wellington came to tell us Helen was awake. Was there anything further you wanted to ask me?"

"No, but I would like to talk to Tinker again if she's around. First, though, I need to powder my nose."

My curiosity over what Lola had given me had to be satisfied before I could carry on productive conversation. I noticed few details about the bathroom to which the secretary pointed me, a few doors down the hall. Judging by its size, and the fact it held three separate vanity sinks, each with mirrored medicine cabinet, I surmised it served several family members. Reaching into my pocket, I took out the item from Helen's chum.

It was a calling card. An ordinary calling card. The edge was raised, and the name Lola Price executed in fine engraving. All the same, it was a disappointment.

Hoping there was something written on the back, I turned it over. Bingo. A phone number. Lola's, I presumed.

She had written it ahead of time rather than scribble it down on the spot. Why? Because she didn't want Helen to know about the communication.

One of the women who claimed to have no secrets from each other did.

I flushed the commode and ran some water, then went out to join Kaye.

"I saw Tinker heading outside just before you arrived," she reported. "She'll probably be on the terrace. She's fond of reading out there."

She led the way down a hall toward a side door next to the kitchen. Midway there a set of French doors led to a flagstone terrace with lounge chairs, several small tables, and another that was long enough to seat ten people. The low brick wall enclosing the terrace held bowl shaped flowerpots in which tulips and late blooming daffodils showed off their color. Tinker Barrett sat on one of the lounges with a nearby umbrella shading the book on her lap.

"If you don't mind being left on your own..." Kaye made vague brushing motions in Tinker's direction. "I have things I should attend to."

She ducked back into the house before I could answer.

I sauntered toward the pixielike young woman under the umbrella. She didn't look up. She wore trousers and a matching sweater set, and the clothes looked as though they'd been chosen for comfort rather than style, which surprised me a little. When I stopped just inches away from her and she still made no move to acknowledge my presence, I pretended not to notice she was pretending not to notice me.

"I've got a bone to pick with you," I said.

She turned a page.

"I'm wondering," I continued as if she'd responded, "why when I talked to you last night you didn't say anything about how Arlene reacted when Charlotte came down with her suitcase."

"Maybe because she wasn't around." Tinker slammed her book closed. "She left right after lunch. Why? What's going on?"

"Funny, she claims she was in here with you, looking at magazines. She mentioned the same things you did." Even more details, I thought, recalling her description of Jack smacking the wall. I'd told enough whoppers myself to know embellishment was a good way to sell them. "So. Which one of you is telling the truth?"

Tinker swung her feet to the ground, her eyes a storm front of anger.

"We had a spat that morning. Arlene and I. She's a brat if you argue with her. She hardly said two words to me at lunch. She'd have been as likely to go downtown in rags as to be in the same room with me that afternoon."

Her account didn't fit the picture of a congenial noonday gathering everyone else had painted. It was veering off the road on several counts, all or which I could check.

"What was the spat about?"

She flung her hand in dismissal. "Nothing to do with any of this."

"With Charlotte."

Today instead of the bangle bracelet she'd toyed with last night, a gold charm bracelet decorated her wrist. One of the charms had caught in the cuff of her sweater. She gave it an angry yank. "Right."

For the first time in this back and forth, her eyes avoided mine.

"It was over a joke, okay? A stupid practical joke. Nothing important."

She got to her feet, preparing to leave. I stepped in front of her. We both knew I wouldn't physically stop her here in this mansion of privilege.

"It's bothering you, though. That's why you're fixing to run."

"It had nothing to do with Charlotte's getting killed!"

"You might feel better getting it off your chest."

"Fine then. The day before the accident, the three of us were going to the country club for lunch. Arlene had this idea, and I gave her one of my bracelets. While we were all dressing, she took it in to Charlotte and told her I didn't want the bracelet anymore and she could have it, that it would look nice with the suit Charlotte was wearing that day.

"When we got to the club and divided up for bridge tables I made sure Charlotte was at the same table as me – looking after her and that. Then when we were playing, I pretended to notice the bracelet and get all upset. I said, 'Is that my bracelet? What are you doing with it?' Of course, she was embarrassed and said Arlene had told her she could have it. Arlene was at the next table over and she said no she hadn't. I guess – I guess I never expected Charlotte to take it as hard as she did. It was all she could do not to cry with everyone staring at her.

"She was miffed on the way home, but she didn't say anything and neither did we. I thought it would just blow over. She seemed okay the next morning. I tried to make it up to her, though. I told her there were no hard feelings, and I was glad to lend her things if she just asked."

"In other words, you tried to make it look like it was all Arlene's doing."

"Well, yes, and it was Arlene's idea. But it didn't

matter, because Charlotte told me off. She said she didn't for a minute believe I knew nothing about it, that Arlene and I were both little back stabbers. I sort of lost my temper. When she talked back like that. I said maybe I just didn't like thieves, and that nothing else better go missing because nobody else in the family would let it go like I had."

It was warm there on the sunny patio, but I felt a chill. A mean-spirited trick, followed by angry words, had sent a young woman running off to her death.

But no.

There must be more to it.

What I'd heard so far wasn't enough to make Charlotte fear for her life.

Two women in ruffled white aprons came out and snapped a blue tablecloth into perfection on the long table. Another woman deposited a stack of plates and napkins and distributed them.

"She seemed fine at lunch," Tinker said defensively. "Okay, so maybe she gave us the silent treatment. Sometimes she didn't say much anyway. Even when she came downstairs to leave I thought she was just going for her afternoon walk like always until I saw she had her suitcase."

While I was still absorbing her words about an afternoon walk, Tinker swept around me into the house. Twice in the course of one conversation she'd upended what I thought I knew.

***

Returning to the house, I nearly collided with Kaye in the hallway.

"Oh, sorry!" She gave an embarrassed titter. "Did you talk to everyone you wanted to?"

"No, and now they're setting up for lunch." I said more curtly than she deserved.

"You're more than welcome to join us."

"No thanks. Where's Arlene?"

"I believe she's gone out with her friend Pammy. They're like a pair of puppies, always romping around together."

"Does Pammy have a last name?"

"Witherspoon." Kaye became flustered. "I'm sorry, I thought it was only Tinker and some of the staff you wanted to speak to. The housekeeper's free now. She's not involved in lunch preparations."

"Thanks." I forced civility back into my manner. Kaye so far had been a valuable resource. "I do have one quick question though before you go on your way."

"Yes?"

"I understand Charlotte took a walk every day."

"Unless it was raining."

"When?"

"After lunch. She said it helped the digestion. I thought perhaps she just needed a break from us and that was her nice way of going about it."

"Who knew she went walking?"

Kaye frowned. "Everyone, I suppose. Wouldn't you say, Judith?"

Simon's secretary had come into the hallway, probably on her way to lunch and the break from work matters which she'd lauded earlier.

"Who knew… Oh. Yes. I suppose everyone. In a general way, at least. The men may have been unaware, their minds are so taken up with work. What a relief if this progress the allies are making is actually the end to the war."

It had the absent ring of something one was expected to say. As with the men she worked with, her mind was elsewhere.

Kaye had already vanished. Now, with a smile, Judith brushed past me, headed for the deceptively sunny patio.

CHAPTER THIRTEEN

Mrs. Randall, the housekeeper, was a sour old soul. She and the cook had been planning menus when Charlotte died. The boy who got fired got no more than a thief deserved. His first name was Jimmy, and his last name was "something Frenchie sounding." She'd have to get out her record books for previous years to look it up. I told her I would appreciate it, and asked to speak to the girl who had tidied up Charlotte's room after she left. The housekeeper's martyred sign left me debating which I found more unpleasant to deal with, her or Tinker.

The rosy-cheeked maid she sent to talk to me was named Janine. She looked to be all of sixteen and wide-eyed, currently verging on wild-eyed.

"What can you tell me about how Miss Littlefield's room looked after she left?"

"Nothing," she said, her voice just above a whisper.

"Nothing?"

"Just like she'd left in a hurry. There were some hangers on the floor. She'd left some nice dresses. And-and she'd thrown out some face powder."

"Thrown it out?"

She nodded. "In the wastebasket," she said in her semi-whisper. Her eyes dipped.

"Did you check the drawers? See if she'd left anything?"

"Yes. I'm supposed to after visitors. She hadn't, and if anybody says different or that I took anything, they're lying!"

Bursting into tears, she ran out of the closet-sized room off the kitchen where we'd been talking. Finding her and smoothing her feathers took fifteen minutes, which put Mrs. Randall out of sorts with both of us.

***

As much as I wanted to know why Lola Price had slipped me her phone number, I felt a greater need to know why Arlene had lied to me about her whereabouts on the afternoon Charlotte died and where she'd really been. What I didn't want to do was make others in the household aware of the discrepancy. Nor did I want to stick around until Kaye finished lunch and could give me the address of Arlene's friend Pammy.

On the off chance Jack was in what had been the library prior to its conversion into his wartime office, and that he wasn't on the phone, I detoured to check.

He was at his desk, skimming a stack of papers in front of him and scribbling on a notepad. He looked up at my tap on his half-open door.

"Have you found something?"

"I'm not sure yet. I was hoping you could tell me the address for Pamela Witherspoon's family."

Giving a small chuckle, he returned his fountain pen to its desk stand.

"Pamela. I don't think I've ever heard her called by her full name before. Is it Pammy you want to reach or her parents? She doesn't live at home. She has her own apartment, over on Park Drive."

"Her own apartment? Why?"

"Because she has a grandfather who buys her anything her parents won't. And since she has her own place of residence, she can also have her own car." For the first time since I'd met him, he looked amused. "I suspect that's part of the appeal for my sister."

"The car?"

"The freedom." He sighed. "To be fair, I'm sure it's boring for Arlene with everyone else around here working all day. Mother can't do things with her. She and Tinker spend time together, but they get tired of each other. She should have stayed in college. She's smart. But she made such a stink about going back for her junior year that Dad gave in. He'd just brought Mother home. He was already running a business, and the war work they're doing adds to the pressure. He didn't – doesn't – have time to be a parent as well."

Frowning, he looked at me more closely.

"Why this interest in Pammy? You can't think she had anything to do with what happened to Charlotte."

"It sounds as if she's here a lot. I thought she might be able to shed some light on what happened. Noticed something, heard something."

"Oh." Apparently that satisfied him. "Well, I won't deny Pammy's spoiled, but she's okay. Our families have known each other forever. Arlene needs a friend, and she could do worse, I suppose, even though Pammy's a snot at times and... well, in my eyes at least... shallow. What mystifies me is why Pammy, who's three years older and has plenty of friends in her own crowd, has become such pals with my sister."

The phone at his elbow rang. He picked it up.

"Cuba? I can't hear – Yes. Yes, go ahead."

He was no longer aware of my presence.

***

Pammy Witherspoon's apartment was too far south and east of downtown to be fashionable, but in a neighborhood that was safe and pleasant. It was at the front of a three-story, twelve-unit brownstone.

On my way there I stopped at a diner where I had a plate of fairly decent red-flannel hash and used the directory next to the pay phone to look up Pammy's address. At any rate there was a P.L. Witherspoon listed at an address that sounded likely. To make sure I was right, I called first.

"Pamela?" I inquired in a pinched voice.

"Who's asking?"

"I'm calling about a little problem we seem to be having with your account."

I'd plucked it out of thin air, something less likely to make her take off than if I'd simply hung up the phone. I expected either confusion or indignant denial.

"Yeah? Well, tell that creep he'll get what I owe him. Tell him he doesn't scare me, so he can save his breath – or maybe it's your breath – and not bother trying."

I held the receiver away from my ear just in time to save my eardrum. A customer on the stool at the end of the counter, who had heard the irritated voice on the other end, if not the words, turned to look.

"Wrong number." I shrugged as I hung up.

The problem-with-your-account ploy usually caused people to think of their bank, or a store credit account. This time I'd gotten more than I'd bargained for. Hoping my call hadn't prompted Pammy to make herself scarce, I paid for my hash and drove directly there. A triangular face in a cloud of pale blond hair peered out at me.

"I need to give Arlene a message. Is she here?"

"A message? For me?" Arlene squeezed up behind her friend. "It's that detective Jack hired."

"She's not a real detective. I don't have to let her in." Pammy started to close the door.

"Wait!" protested Arlene.

I shoved the door back as far as the chain would allow.

"I'm real enough to have a license signed by the chief of police. Real enough to get you in hot water if I tell your grandpa about the money you owe."

"Is it Mother? Has something happened to Mother? Let her in, Pammy!"

With a snort to show her displeasure, Pammy Witherspoon stepped aside. Her triangular face hinted foxlike cunning as she assessed me. The waves of her pale hair brought to mind Lana Turner and Veronica Lake. Whereas Arlene had the sort of all-American girl beauty that drew wolf whistles, Pammy exuded the pinup girl sultriness of which starlets were made.

"Grandpop's butler wouldn't give you the time of day," she sneered.

I pointed a silencing finger at her. "You don't interest me. It's Arlene I'm here to see."

"What's happened? What's wrong?"

The quaver in the girl's voice made me feel a faint

scrap of guilt. "Your mother's fine. The message is from me. Namely that I don't like being lied to."

"I didn't—"

"Yes, you did." I noted the living room, which a decorator with a very large budget had graced with dainty French style furniture and fragile bits of china. The garments discarded here and there were, I surmised, Pammy's way of adding a homey touch. "You told me you were looking at magazines with Tinker when Charlotte ran out with her suitcase. You weren't."

"Tinker's the one who's lying! To-to get me in trouble."

"You weren't with Tinker. You weren't even in the house when Charlotte left, or when she was killed. Where were you?"

"I... I..."

"It's okay." Pammy sauntered forward. "We might as well come clean."

"But you said—"

"She was with me." Pammy slid an arm around Arlene's waist. "We were hostessing at a U.S.O. canteen." She gave Arlene a reassuring little shake.

Arlene swallowed.

I looked at the pair of them standing there. Both were the very nth of fashion in their slacks, blouses and bracelets. Behind them, remnants of two cigarettes were burning out in a large china ashtray.

Half a dozen tubes of lipstick around the ashtray suggested they'd been trying colors. These weren't girls I could picture volunteering to chat with homesick soldiers they'd never met.

"Which one?" I asked.

"What?"

"Which U.S.O. canteen where?"

"Oh. Over on Linden. I don't know the address."

I looked at Arlene, who hadn't said a word so far and was chewing the edge of her lip. "Why would you lie about something like that?"

"Because I asked her to and she was being a pal," Pammy answered. The slits of her own eyes didn't look very pal-like just then. She wrinkled her nose with an art she'd probably practiced in front of a mirror. "Grandpop makes me do it. The U.S.O. bit. He's kind of old fashioned, and says I should do my part for the war effort. He's a sweet old thing, so I humor him, but Arlene knows how much I hate it, so she comes with me sometimes."

Arlene nodded vigorously.

"That still doesn't explain why you wanted to hide the fact you were doing it. Lots of young women volunteer as U.S.O. hostesses."

"We'd be... we'd be laughed at if anyone knew!" Arlene found her voice.

"It's fine for girls in the lunch bucket set," said Pammy. "Keeps morale up and that. But we'd be laughed out of every party we went to if word got out that we did it. And you know what?" Removing her arm from Arlene's waist, she sauntered to the coffee table. She lighted a fresh cigarette, inhaled slowly, and shook back her curtain of champagne hair. "Going to that smelly place doesn't make me feel a bit more virtuous."

She blew a smoke ring. "Now if you don't mind, I've got to be somewhere, and drop off Arlene at her house on the way."

I didn't for a minute believe that she had someplace to be, but I'd had all of Pammy Witherspoon I could stomach for the moment. With a smile which I hoped was smug enough to irritate her, I left.

It was within the realm of possibility that the pair had been at a U.S.O. club. But even telling about it had seemed like too much of a lark to Pammy. I'd bet a week's gas money they were lying about where they'd really been when Charlotte was killed.

CHAPTER FOURTEEN

Lola Price got right to the point when I telephoned.

"You're wondering why I resorted to subterfuge to give you my phone number, and just after Helen and I had declared we had no secrets from each other."

"Something like that."

"I want to give any help I can. I don't want to lose Helen's trust if I do. I don't believe the first necessarily merits the second, do you?"

Instead of answering her question, I asked one of my own. "What kind of help?"

"I've known the family intimately for years – the foibles of each, and what makes them tick. But I have, I think, the objectivity of an outsider. I can connect names that come up, or have come up, to people and their history with the Barretts."

It could go a long way toward helping me penetrate the rarefied world occupied by my primary suspects. It could also be a time when looking in a gift horse's mouth was the wise thing to do.

"Does the name Pammy Witherspoon ring a bell?"

The force with which she let her breath out might

as well have been the grinding of teeth. "Not the companion I would have chosen for Arlene, but Helen doesn't object. If you don't mind, I'd rather not talk about this on the phone."

***

Lola lived in one of the nicer apartment buildings north of the river. They were near the art museum, substantial, but not ritzy. The front units in Lola's building looked out on the Great Miami. Lola's apartment was at the rear.

"I apologize if I'm difficult to understand," she said as she let me in. "I've been to the dentist and my lip's a bit puffy."

On the phone, I'd been aware of a slight slur which hadn't been there when I met her that morning, but I thought perhaps she'd had a nip or two at lunch. Having assured her I could understand her perfectly, I took the chair she indicated.

In contrast to the careless disarray of Pammy Witherspoon's place, the room where I now sat was a jewel of both taste and order. The walls were Wedgewood blue. The walnut furniture bore traces of wear, and there was perhaps one more piece of it than a room that size needed, but the effect was charming. A silver tea set too fine for the modest apartment occupied a table in front of the sofa where Lola settled. Stacked neatly by the door through which I'd entered were four library books.

"It's one of the ways I watch pennies." Lola had caught the direction of my eyes. "Library books."

Her voice had a scratchy quality which wasn't unpleasant. I wondered why she had to pinch pennies. "They're a mainstay for me too. That photograph's one of Helen's, isn't it? The willow tree?"

"Yes." Smile lines crinkled at the corner of her eyes as she finished filling a teacup, which she then slid toward me. "If she hadn't had the misfortune of being born into money, I believe her talent would have taken her far." She laughed at my expression. "I come from the same background. I know the constraints it imposes."

"You've known each other since you were girls?"

"No, since we were both young newlyweds. I was an outsider – from Cleveland. Helen befriended me. We moved in the same circles, went to the same events, and we found ourselves drifting off to a corner to talk, really talk."

She took a sip of tea, a bit awkwardly since she turned her mouth to avoid the puffy patch of lip she'd mentioned earlier.

"We've been part of each other's lives for a very long time. When I finally filed for divorce and the philandering rat I'd put up with for twenty years left me with hardly two nickels to rub together, Helen was the only friend who stuck by me. When I wouldn't let her take me to lunch at the country club because I couldn't reciprocate, she said fine, we'd go to little cafes we both could afford, and that's what we did until she got polio. I would crawl over broken glass for Helen – but I'll also tell you the truth about the members of her family."

"Why?"

Lola pursed her lips. "Helen was fond of Charlotte. I think it surprised her as much as it did the girl. When you raised the possibility that Charlotte's death wasn't an accident... She wants to know the truth. No, more than wants, she needs to. Helen has a very strong sense of right and wrong. I know she'll make every attempt to be honest with you, but when it comes to her family, her children in particular, she may have blind spots. What mother wouldn't?"

"Whereas you lack them."

"I believe so. And if I can spare Helen a bit of pain where they're concerned, I would like to."

Her hand rose as if to touch her jaw, then drew away without completing the act. I set my teacup in its saucer.

"Your visit to the dentist is catching up with you. I'll go."

"No, don't. On the phone you intimated you had questions about Pammy Witherspoon. I can answer those at least."

Although I was certain Pammy and Arlene were

lying about some part of their actions the afternoon Charlotte was killed, I wasn't sure how big a whopper they were telling, or why. I wasn't ready to share my doubts about them yet. "You expressed reservations about the friendship between her and Arlene. Any particular reason why?"

Lola shrugged. "Nothing I can put my finger on. It's just... Arlene was a sweet girl until she took up with Pammy. She's not spoiled." She laughed. "Well, perhaps she is, somewhat, but not like Pammy. I doubt Pammy ever thought of anyone but herself in her life."

"Yet Helen, despite her sense of right and wrong you mentioned, doesn't object to the amount of time they spend together?"

Lola sighed. "That's one of the tragedies of Helen's illness. She can't keep an eye on things the way she did. She can't do things with Arlene the way she did. They were quite close. Still are, really. I think that's much of the reason the poor child quit college. She was terrified when Helen fell ill. She wanted to be with her, to be reassured her mother was still alive.

"Arlene got shortchanged on childhood. Her mother was gravely ill, her father's attention was all focused on Helen's wellbeing – and then boom, the war effort suddenly demanded part of that."

Plenty of kids had it rougher, I thought. In fact, compared with many, Arlene's abrupt acquaintance with reality had been a bed of roses.

"So everyone thought 'Oh, isn't it nice that Arlene has a friend,'" I said. "Because, I suppose, her parents knew Pammy's parents, which was enough for her to pass muster."

Something in what I said amused Lola. "They were used to seeing her around. She's two years younger than Jack. They were part of the same crowd at school, at tennis, at dances. Some people, Pammy in particular, expected that she'd marry Jack."

"Why?"

She shrugged. "They knew each other. They shared a similar background. Jack's easy-going and didn't seem inclined to find a girl himself. Marriages have been based on less."

***

What Lola had said about Pammy expecting to marry Jack kept a lock on my thoughts for several hours after I left her. Was her assessment accurate? Did she know the Barrett family as well as she claimed?

Did she know Pammy?

I was willing to give considerable weight to Lola's input. Beneath the surface there was a no nonsense manner about her. It also fit what Audrey, the girl at Mrs. Salmon's place who had visited Charlotte, told about a friend of the Barretts making insulting comments in Charlotte's presence.

If Pammy had expected to marry Jack, it put Pammy and her actions in an altogether different light. For the moment I skipped the fact I couldn't imagine why she would set her sights on Jack in particular. She must know plenty of young men whose bank account equaled his. Did she see him as an especially good candidate for being led around by the nose?

Any suggestion that love was part of the equation was laughable. The impression I'd formed of her at her apartment had only been underscored by Lola's comment that Pammy never thought about anyone but herself. Being hit with the fact Jack intended to marry someone else must have made her furious. As to whether that anger could prompt her to hire someone to run Charlotte over, I wouldn't put money one way or another.

A visit to the U.S.O. club where the girls claimed to have been would help clarify things, but I wanted to go there armed with a photograph of Pammy Witherspoon. Without saying why I wanted it, I had asked Lola if she could get me one. She promised to have it for me the next afternoon.

Her puffy lip was gone and her diction was crisp again when she let me in.

"All the pictures I found of Pammy show her with Arlene, which I suppose makes sense. I have them because they're photos of Arlene." She gave a graceful gesture toward half a dozen four-by-five snapshots spread on her coffee table. "Take your pick."

In two of the photographs the girls seemed to be trying for magazine model poses. I took one of those.

"Did you ask for this because you think Pammy had something to do with Charlotte's death?"

Lola's husky voice had a thread of worry. I suspected she might be entertaining a second thought or two about being a helpful friend.

"I think she may have told a lie that muddied the waters," I said.

***

Photographs in hand, I drove directly to the only U.S.O. I'd found an address for on Linden Avenue. Pammy's claim that it was hard to find was pure bunkum. It occupied what had once been some sort of retail store. The front window which once had displayed shoes or vacuum cleaners or sewing supplies to passersby now featured bunting in red, white, and blue, and insignia for the various armed services. The letters U.S.O. were painted prominently across the front.

At three in the afternoon, the place was nearly empty. A quartet of young G.I.s sat at a corner table playing cards and drinking pop out of bottles.

Another plinked out a tune on an upright piano with chipped keys. Somebody gave a wolf whistle as I entered.

"If you're selling something, we don't have any money. If you want to sit on the bar and swing those legs of yours, you'd be doing your country a service," said the affable fellow behind a counter that served as a bar.

I laughed. "Actually, I'm hoping to find out if you've seen a couple of girls I'm looking for." I handed him a business card and watched his eyebrows rise. "They're not in any trouble, I'm just trying to find out if they were where they claimed to be two weeks ago."

"A lot of girls come in for dances, or to volunteer," he said dubiously.

I slid the picture of Pammy and Arlene across the counter.

"How about these two? They ever help out here?"

A hulking fellow with a missing eye tooth who'd been polishing glasses drifted over to get a look too.

"These gals haven't so much as come through the door," said the one who'd been talking to me. His features crinkled in a roguish grin. "I'd remember, too. That one's a looker."

His pinkie nudged the image of Pammy Witherspoon.

CHAPTER FIFTEEN

What I'd learned about Pammy and Arlene came as no surprise. A small growl of satisfaction might have escaped me as I swung the DeSoto into the parking area at the back of Pammy's apartment building. I'd stopped at the office long enough to call the Barrett place, which netted me the information the girls weren't there. That being the case, I was betting I'd find them here.

Instead, I found nobody home despite my repeated knocking.

After giving myself a lecture on counting my chickens, I settled down in my car to wait. With or without Arlene, Pammy would come home at some point. Half past four was thumbing its nose at me when she finally did so, accompanied by Arlene.

Getting out of my car, I ambled toward them. They were sorting out shopping bags and didn't notice me at first. Then Arlene caught Pammy's sleeve.

"Now what?" Pammy tossed her pale hair to signal impatience.

"Now I tell you they've never seen either one of

you at that U.S.O. club and wait for today's malarkey about where you were."

"On a picnic." Pammy smiled blandly.

"A picnic. Arlene must have some appetite. She'd just finished lunch."

"I couldn't eat anything at home that day. My stomach was all in knots."

"Because of the argument you had with Tinker that morning? I don't blame her for being sore. That was a nasty little trick you played on Charlotte."

"What trick?" Pammy's voice sharpened. "You didn't tell me about any trick."

"It wasn't important."

"I don't suppose you'd like to tell me where this picnic took place?"

"We don't have to. We're both twenty-one. We can go anywhere we please!" Arlene repeated the lines like a good little parrot. The wobble in her voice undermined the effect.

"You're right, you don't have to tell me. The police might see things differently, though, depending on what you told them."

Arlene's face went white.

"Hills and Dales, okay?" Pammy slid a shopping bag from one arm to the other and slammed her car door. "I lied because I don't like you. I don't like people picking on my friend." She gave Arlene's shoulders a squeeze vigorous enough to rattle her teeth. "They ignore her at home unless she zigs when they think she should zag. The poor kid needs to get out, have some fun. And like she said, it's really nobody's business where we go."

I bit my tongue to keep from pointing out that it mattered in what could turn into a murder investigation.

"I don't suppose anyone might remember seeing you there," I said instead.

"There was an old lady there with a couple of brats. Grandma, probably. Maybe she goes every day. Or..." Pammy smirked. "There's a pudgy little guy who lives at the end of the hall. He'd lost his job that day – got laid off so some G.I. who'd been sent home with missing toes and used to work there could have it. He was feeling blue so we took him along.

"He's not home," she said as my eyes traveled to the apartment building. "It's the day he does something with a rowing club and then has dinner at his sister's. He'll be at my place around nine if you want to talk to him. I'm having some friends in for drinks, so park back here to leave the spaces in front for them. His name's Arnold, by the way."

***

There wasn't enough of the day left to merit going back to my office. At home, in comfortable clothes and socks that had been darned several times, I stretched out on my bed and contemplated the evening ahead. The fluffy white kitten who had joined the household at Christmastime stretched out on my chest and purred background music.

The kitten had been my gift to Seamus who had said one night that all we needed to make our house just about perfect was a cat. 'A little fluffy white one.' One of the detectives roomed with an old woman at the edge of town, and every time I'd been there, she'd had a litter of kittens living under her porch. The one I found had a patch of golden yellow on one ear and the side of her muzzle. Seamus had christened her Toffee, because, he said, she looked like she'd stuck her head in a toffee pot.

As her purring subsided, my thoughts returned to Pammy and Arlene, and the growing collection of stories they'd attempted to get me to swallow. Pammy probably thought she was clever, offering me one of her chums who would swear to the truth of whatever tale she'd told me. What she might not realize was that in giving me access to one guest at tonight's little party, she'd also given me access to the rest. They might not be willing to talk to me, but there was a chance I would hear, or see, something useful.

At a quarter to nine, I turned into the little parking lot where I'd surprised Pammy and Arlene that afternoon. If the witness Pammy had so smugly offered didn't show up because he didn't exist, she couldn't very well throw me out until the time had come and gone for him to be there. Meanwhile, I'd have a chance to eavesdrop.

Then again, I had a feeling there was no predicting what Pammy might do.

Years of coming and going at hours when other women were tucked up at home knitting or reading, and in neighborhoods where they wouldn't venture in daylight, had made checking my surroundings second nature. No shadows moved. No bushes provided a spot from which someone could pounce on a person heading up the short driveway leading to the front of the building. What I was mostly alert for, though I didn't expect to hear it as I got out of my car, was the sound of a car engine revving to rush toward me like the one that had mown down Charlotte.

The night was silent. As I rounded the rear of my car, I was weighing whether Arlene or Pammy or both had done something two weeks ago which they now felt the need to hide with a lie.

The shoulder slamming into my knees came with no warning.

I went down hard on my backside. I rolled, but not in time to keep my assailant from landing a halfway decent punch on my face, which I reciprocated with a better one. A few more back-and-forths made it clear that while he had strength on his side, I had more skill. When an opening presented itself, I kneed him in the gut, his more sensitive regions being out of reach. In response, he grabbed me by the hair and yanked me to my knees.

"Quit meddling!" he snapped.

As he flipped my head back against the fender of my DeSoto, I managed to free my .38 from its holster at the small of my back. The teeth rattling meeting of my skull with metal left me momentarily stunned, but not too stunned to realize when he jerked me forward on my knees that he meant to do it again. I fired in the general direction of his feet.

A yelp rewarded me. I fell sideways as he released me. He took off running. Catching myself on my elbow, I looked up in time to see him jump into a car. The engine roared and it screeched away without lights.

The whole episode had probably taken less than a minute, no more than two. I sat for a minute, panting, with my back against the rear wheel of my DeSoto.

My attacker must have been crouching down between cars where spotting him would be unlikely. When I pulled in and headed for a parking spot, he'd run along behind my car and waited. He couldn't have been very old, mid-thirties or under to be that agile. Was it one of Pammy's pals? Someone she'd hired to welcome me? The same person who had run over Charlotte?

Pammy and Arlene were the only two people who expected me to come here tonight. Arlene could just as easily be the instigator. I didn't like that prospect, but I had to consider it.

Pushing to my feet, I dusted my skirt. Regardless of which girl was behind the attack, they wouldn't expect me to show up at Pammy's door afterward, so that's precisely what I intended to do.

***

Music was blaring away when I knocked on the door of Pammy's apartment. No one came to see what I wanted. I may have knocked a little too loudly the second time. The door behind me flew open.

"She's not here." A gray haired man scowled out at me. "She and a bunch went out about an hour ago."

A woman I took to be his wife wiggled in beside him. "Pushed past us without saying 'pardon me' or even nodding."

They didn't appear to be fans of Pammy. I gave them a card. The man's scowl smoothed out and his eyebrows raised. His wife made a cooing sound.

"What can you tell me about Miss Witherspoon?"

"Nothing except she's rude as can be and runs around all the time," said the man. He looked at his wife.

"Well... I think she might have a younger sister. I

see her a lot with another girl who looks younger and, well, not quite as hard. Has she done something?"

"Told a fib or two that might get someone in trouble."

"Oh, dear!"

"Does anyone named Arnold live on this floor?"

"At the end of the hall. Arnold James."

They watched as I knocked on his door. If they weren't comparing notes with him two minutes after I left, they would be tomorrow.

Arnold James answered the door in his stocking feet. He was a plump young fellow with dewy cheeks and a friendly manner. I introduced myself and told him I was doing a background check.

"Could you tell me the date of the picnic you went on with Pammy Witherspoon and a friend of hers named Arlene Barrett?"

His mouth gave a series of jerks before he lost the battle and gurgled with laughter.

"The snotty little blond who lives up the hall? She wouldn't give me the time of day, much less invite me along on a picnic. Is this some kind of joke?"

CHAPTER SIXTEEN

My mirror the next morning allowed no dispute that I had a shiner. I'd had worse, but this one was nasty enough. Its dark blue was hard to distinguish from black. The cold bottle of beer I'd held against it when I got home last night had soothed my bruised flesh, but it hadn't stopped the swelling much. A quarter-inch slit permitting partial vision between my eyelids said more about my attacker than about my medical skills.

I thought about that on the way to my office, then thought about it some more once I'd gone through the mail and settled in with a fresh tablet in front of me. Its ruled sheets helped me order my thoughts.

Whoever had jumped me last night had known how to punch, but not how to fight. Judging by the speed with which he'd fled once I fired off a shot, he'd gotten more than he bargained for. Those things suggested he hadn't been an experienced thug, but was more likely some pal of Pammy's. Not necessarily, though.

Pammy might have been content to invite me to a

non-existent party and then take off, leaving me with nothing to show for my efforts while she enjoyed a good laugh. It suited what I'd seen of her personality. Arlene had heard her issue the invitation, however, including instructions to park in back. If she was the one with something to hide, she, too, might have a male acquaintance willing to knock me around until he discovered I fought back. And if Arlene had mentioned it to anyone else at the Barrett house – say she and Tinker had made up – any number of people could have taken advantage of the situation.

Bringing my palms together, I blew through my fingers. Because it had been so cloudy last night, and because my attacker wore some sort of filmy fabric over his face, identification on that score was impossible. The best I could do was eliminate members of the Barrett household as possible suspects. Simon was too short and too old for the nimbleness of the man in the parking lot. Jack, in addition to his impaired gait, was too tall. Noah was a possibility. So, it occurred to me, was Simon's nail biting assistant John McDowell.

Considering either man necessitated consideration of motive for them as well. My gray matter had already exercised plenty for one stretch, so I got out the phone book and looked up the place where Pammy's neighbor Arnold James had told me he worked. He'd even provided his supervisor's name. I felt certain Pammy's whole tale about him and the picnic had been a lie, and I was right.

"Mr. James hasn't missed a day of work since January," his supervisor assured me. "He had a bout of flu, as I recall."

"He wasn't laid off recently?"

"Laid off? Goodness no. Why would he be?"

***

It was time to have a little heart-to-heart with Arlene. The best chance to talk to her without Pammy was to catch her at home before lunch, I reasoned. It was mid-morning, time for all but the worst carousers to be up and about. Or so I thought.

"I'm sorry, Miss Barrett is indisposed this morning," Griggs informed me.

I raised an eyebrow. Was the girl hung over, or had she anticipated I might come by?

"Hello. Are you here to see Helen?" Kaye descended the stairs with an open notebook in one hand. She came to a halt at the bottom. "Goodness! Your poor eye! What happened?"

"An accident. Nothing serious."

Griggs retreated.

"Um, well, let me give Cook this list with a few things Helen wants added to the next grocery order and I'll take you up."

"It's Arlene I wanted to see, but I understand she's not feeling well."

The secretary's long face softened with sympathy. "She gets terrible cramps when it's that time of month, poor kid."

"In fact, she had them two weeks ago." Judith, who had come into the area at the foot of the stairs where we were talking, made no effort to hide her disgust. She addressed herself to Kaye now.

"Where's the business car? Mr. McDowell needs to run an errand for Simon and there's no sign of it, or of Hays either."

"He took it for gas. He's rather unhappy about how much has been used."

Kaye's head made a pointed turn in my direction. "I have to get this list to Cook. I'll be back."

Judith watched her with irritation. "Arlene gets away with far too much – I say as someone with no children." Her smile of self-acknowledgment was stiff. "Simon tries to put his foot down, but—" She stopped. "I'm being indiscreet." Her gaze swept up the stairs. "Arlene's room is the last one on the right. If you're inclined."

***

Arlene's response to my soft knock at her door didn't sound like that of someone in pain.

"Come in for heaven's sake. Are you being—?"

She shot bolt upright at sight of me, or as upright as lounging in bed with a pile of pillows at her back would allow.

"How did...? Get out. I thought you were someone else."

The embroidered pink satin pajamas she wore showed nary a wrinkle. They set off her blond hair, which was shiny from brushing and tied back with a ribbon.

"Gee," I said coming to stand by her bedside with hands on my hips. "People will be glad to know you're feeling lots better than they thought."

To her credit, she didn't try to deny it. All her attention was riveted on my shiner. "Did that... did you get that last night? At— at—"

"What do you think?"

"Oh, God!" Tumbling sideways, she drew her knees up and clutched a pillow to her chest. Tears that had a fifty-fifty chance of being genuine leaked from beneath her closed eyes. "I didn't know... All Pammy planned was to be gone by the time you showed up expecting to find a party. That's all she said anyway. She said you deserved a lesson, that you needed to know you couldn't push us around—"

"Stop sniveling." I rammed the side of her mattress with my knee. "I don't care if your belly's ready to split, which I don't for a minute believe it is by the way, I want the truth. Either tell me where you were when Charlotte was killed, or I'll bring your mother in here to see that you do. Or your father."

She sat up again, her face gone white. "No! Don't bring Mother into this! Please don't. I can't tell you where we were. It would get Pammy in trouble. It had nothing to do with Charlotte, okay? We didn't do anything wrong, but Pammy needed to go somewhere and she wanted me for moral support and-and it would hurt Mother so much if she knew."

If it was an act, she belonged on stage. A thought slowly dawned. "Arlene... did you go somewhere because Pammy is pregnant?"

"What? No. No!"

The horror on her face gave me my first hope she might have at least a smidgen of her mother's sense of right and wrong. Before I could get my next question out, the door swung open.

"Here you are. Cinnamon toast and coffee with half a cow's worth of cream in it to cheer you—"

Tinker stopped as she saw me. The tray in her hands tipped precariously. "What's she doing here? I gave Griggs explicit orders not to let anyone bother you."

"Which he followed," I assured. "Someone else sent me up."

It wasn't exactly the truth, but it wasn't a lie either. I liked to think that put me a few steps ahead of Arlene.

Tinker looked around for the closest place to

deposit the tray. The top of Arlene's white dressing table was too densely populated with discarded jewelry, tubes of lipstick and perfume atomizers. Plopping the tray on the foot of the bed, and looking extremely peeved, she faced me.

"How dare you come in here and browbeat her – again – when she's sick."

"There's nothing wrong with her. You know it; I know it."

Arlene herself didn't say a word. With eyes downcast, she was nudging the book she'd been reading as if it were vital to make it align with her outstretched legs. I gritted my teeth. With someone else around, there was no hope Arlene would tell me anything useful.

"I'm glad to see the two of you have patched things up after your quarrel," I said, and left with a calm which seemed to surprise them.

The book which Arlene had been aligning, the one she'd been reading when I arrived, had been a chemistry text.

CHAPTER SEVENTEEN

Even though Arlene still hadn't told me where she was the afternoon of the hit-skip, I'd learned a thing or two. I'd learned she and Pammy had done something which would embarrass them, or at least Arlene, if people knew. I'd learned Helen's opinion mattered to Arlene. I'd learned she was starting to feel stirrings of guilt, or maybe just worry the truth would come out. Finally, if I chose to believe it, which I did, I'd learned Arlene had been unaware of plans for an attack on me.

The unfolding story wasn't that of two young women covering up a murder. It was one of them doing something stupid because they were spoiled and bored. Or was there more to it than that? In leaving, or in their misadventure, had they witnessed something pertinent to Charlotte's death?

The prints from the film in Charlotte's camera hadn't been ready when I stopped to pick them up the previous day. I walked over and got them, shuffling through them for a quick look as I stood by the counter. I took them back to the office for closer study, but this didn't prove any more useful.

One picture showed Helen, laughing. It was on the dark side, without much contrast. Underexposed, as Helen had said. There were quite a few pictures of Jack, some blurry and most of them taken outside. There was one of Arlene and Tinker, which was sad when you knew how they'd treated her.

The last picture from the roll was so dark I couldn't even make out what it was. There was a vertical shaft of something faintly pale surrounded by darkness. The pale part flared some at the top and tapered toward the bottom. Possibly a table leg, though I wouldn't swear to it. Whatever it was meant to show, I had the sense that it was taken inside. However that, too, was conjecture.

My phone rang. I tossed the photos aside and answered.

"This is Dora," said a woman who could hardly contain her excitement. "You talked to my husband and me last night about that snip Miss Witherspoon."

My sore eye throbbed. "Yes, I remember."

"Well, we got the impression from you that she might be up to no good, so I thought you might want to know there was just quite a fracas over there."

"What kind of fracas?"

"Pounding at her door – I thought it might be the police."

"It wasn't, I take it?"

"No. I only peeked out because I was nervous."

"Of course. Did you see who it was?"

"Oh, yes. It was one of the young fellows who's over there a lot – part of her crowd. But he was hopping mad, shouting that she'd never told him he'd be shot at. Shot at! He was limping, too. Using a crutch anyway. Should I call the police?"

My grin could have put a monkey to shame. "No, ah, I wouldn't worry about it. What did Miss Witherspoon do?"

"Told him to stop being a ninny and yanked him inside. You're sure I shouldn't call the police?"

"No, no. He probably went somewhere he shouldn't have doing an errand for her."

It took several minutes to persuade the helpful neighbor that she wasn't living across from a robbery ring or other nefarious enterprise run by Pammy. By the time I hung up, I decided I'd earned a sandwich at the Arcade. My black eye drew more than a few looks from passersby. Afterward, I set out to do a few background checks for my regular clients. At the second one, the woman I needed to talk to had trouble keeping her gaze away from my face and kept asking me to repeat things. I walked toward Main Street wondering whether my appearance just now was too big a distraction to get anything useful done that afternoon.

"I sure hope you gave the other guy a worse souvenir to remember you by," said a voice at my elbow.

I grinned at the stocky man with bushy eyebrows now strolling beside me. "I think I might have shot one of his toes off," I said. "At minimum he'll be hunting a new pair of shoes. How you doing, Ab?"

"Better than you by the looks of it."

Abner Simms was in charge of security at Rike's department store. I'd worked under him my last two years there, though my designation, and the pay that went with it, was still floorwalker.

"What are you doing out and about in the middle of the day? You get fired?"

"Took the morning off to play golf." He pantomimed hitting a golf ball. "Great game. Outdoors, fresh air. You should try it. You'd be surprised how whacking that little white ball gets rid of aggravation."

"So does shooting jerks," I said.

He laughed. "Any chance I've caught you at the right moment to sweet talk you into working for me again?"

"I'm flattered, Ab. You know that. But no. I like what I do, bruises and all."

"At least walk back with me so I can fix you up with some cucumber slices from one of the restaurants. They'll take that swelling down for you. My kid brother was an amateur boxer who lost more fights than he won. Mother swore by cucumber. She said buying them when they weren't in season just about ate up her food budget, but she'd slap a slice or two on him when he got home, and by morning he'd look almost human."

I had only fond memories of the big department store where I'd started part time while in high school and worked until I set out on my own as a private eye. We went in the Main Street entrance and up to the cafeteria where we yakked about old times and caught up on recent ones. When I left, I had half a dozen thick slices of cucumber wrapped up in a cloth napkin. I ate one of them on the way home.

***

Ab's mother was right about the magical powers of cucumber. My eye was mostly open the next morning. Possibly even better, much of the bruising had faded.

When I got to the office, a peek in the mirror of my compact reassured me my improved looks weren't a figment of my imagination. Once again, the mail held nothing from Heebs. As I considered how to organize my day, it organized itself. My phone rang.

"This is Mrs. Randall, the Barretts' housekeeper," the voice on the other end announced. "The man you were asking about, the one who got fired for stealing, his name's in the paper this morning. Page three. He's the one they found shot in the back of the head."

CHAPTER EIGHTEEN

I grabbed for the paper.

We got one at home now, but most of the time I only read the war news as I wolfed down my breakfast. On most days I bought copies of both local papers from a street seller on the way to my office. My fingers had barely touched the top one when the housekeeper informed me she had things to do and hung up. The phone call had taken about as long as it took me to read the two-inch column of type to which she'd alerted me.

The dead man's name was Jimmy Delozier. He'd been found face down in a field along the Great Miami. Two high school lovebirds walking home along the riverbank had discovered the body.

While the small block of print didn't precisely say they were lovebirds, it was the only reason I could think of for two students to be walking down there as late as they must have been. Both the brevity of the story and its placement told me the paper had gotten wind of it just before the presses ran for the early edition. My brain cells were bubbling away at the idea two individuals connected to the Barretts had died violently in such a short time. The smell produced by that fermentation wasn't pleasant.

I dialed the first number for Lieutenant Freeze in the detective section, then thought better of it. Returning the handset to its cradle I let the rotary click back to zero. If Freeze wasn't aware yet that Delozier had worked for the Barretts, it might be smart to learn some things I wanted to know, which he might be reluctant to let me have once he was. I called the housekeeper back.

"Now what?" she asked when she came to the phone. She didn't sound pleased.

"You said you had a record of him in some ledger. Did you find it? Did it have an address for him?"

"It wasn't a matter of finding it. It was getting it down. And I wrote the address out to give you before I saw that business in the paper."

"Is it where you can put your hands on it? No, wait." I interrupted her sigh. "I'll be right over."

The reaction that news of Delozier's death produced in other household members might be worth seeing. It might shake loose other tidbits, too.

This time I decided to approach the imposing mansion from the rear, through the servants' entrance. The household staff would have been the ones who knew the dead man best. With the news of Delozier's death stirring recollection and speculation, that was where I was most likely to hear something interesting. The Barretts themselves could wait a bit.

A harassed looking maid opened the door when I knocked.

"Oh," she said looking me over. "You want Mrs. Randall. You'll have to wait till she finishes ripping the butcher boy's head off for bringing tough chops yesterday." We went through a door to the kitchen and she indicated a chair. "Over there."

On the far side of the room, the housekeeper was upbraiding a young delivery boy so fiercely that he was bending backwards.

"Gee," I said to the maid, whose chores or manners were taking her a few steps with me, "what's it like to know somebody who got shot in the head like that guy who worked here?"

"He was before my time. I think the only ones around who knew him are the bosses."

She left me to make my way to the chair, which was next to the china pantry. Two maids were working inside. One handed down a stack of plates, followed by one of saucers, to another girl who set them on a wooden countertop. The scrape and slap of a whisk kept a staccato beat in a bowl held by a Negro woman who, judging by her apron and her air of authority, was the cook. The housekeeper sent the butcher boy on his way and came toward me.

"I'd already copied down his name and address for

next time you came." She handed me a folded sheet of paper with tidy script.

"Thanks." I looked at it long enough to get the address, then slipped it into my purse. "That must have been kind of a shock, looking up someone who used to work here in your records and then opening the paper to read that about him."

"I wouldn't have seen it if it weren't for Mr. Hays."

"The chauffeur?"

"Nobody else with that name works here. He came trotting in and stuck his folded up paper under my nose before we'd finished putting out the family breakfast. Asked me if it was the same James Delozier who used to work here. I didn't know what he was talking about. I don't read articles with lurid headlines."

The so-called headline hadn't been much bigger than body type and consisted only of *Homicide* or maybe *Homicide Victim.*

"I can't say I'm surprised," the housekeeper added. "Even when he was here, you could see he was going to be trouble. Goodness knows what sort of people he ran afoul of."

"What sort of trouble?"

"Thieving. Lying. Always pretended to be so polite, but turn your back and petty cash came up short or a cigarette lighter went missing. When those two silver cake forks disappeared, and fell out of his pocket when I told him to take off his jacket, that was the last straw."

"You fired him on the spot?"

"Of course not. I can't take it on myself to do something like that. And usually Mr. Griggs would be the one to do the firing if he got instructions to, but he was busy supervising the setup of offices for Mr. Barrett and them while Mr. Barrett spent time at the hospital with Mrs. Barrett, so it fell to me. I didn't mind one bit doing it, either."

The rhythmic slap of the whisking had stopped. The two maids left the pantry, their chatter ceasing as they noticed the housekeeper. Mrs. Randall showed signs of moving on to her duties.

"One last question," I said. "Who told you to fire Delozier?"

She thought a minute.

"Mrs. Price. Mrs. Barrett was too ill to even be thinking of household matters. The doctors weren't sure she'd pull through when she first went into the hospital. Mr. Barrett had too much on his mind to bother him with something like that. Mrs. Price is like part of the family, and used to run a big household herself. She'd come by to get some fancy face cream Mrs. Barrett was wanting. I told her about the forks and asked what should I do. She said fire him, so that's what I did."

***

"I understand you were on better terms with Jimmy Delozier than the rest of the people he worked with," I said to Hays when I tracked him down in the smaller of two garages in back of the Barrett house.

The chauffeur snorted. His uniform jacket hung on a peg. He wore coveralls over the rest of his clothes to protect them as he cleaned the interior of what looked like a spotless car.

"If you mean I worked with the lazy sneak more than the house staff did, then I guess I qualify. Couldn't turn my back on him without him slacking off, and I'd bet a bundle he swiped a wrench of mine that went missing."

"Yet you hotfooted it in to spread the word this morning when you read he'd been killed."

Flushing with embarrassment he tossed aside a cloth he'd been using. "I only told Mrs. Randall. I didn't want her or Griggs to be caught cold if some newspaper called, and I guess maybe I told her because it threw me some, reading it. I didn't like Delozier, but it's not the sort of thing you expect, somebody you've worked with getting shot in the head like in a pulp novel."

"Did you see him or talk to him after he got fired?"

"Two months back or thereabouts he had the nerve to come around asking did I need a helper again. I told him to get lost." He hesitated. "I guess maybe that was part of it hitting me so, reading that he'd been killed. Relief that I hadn't had anything to do with him. Shot in the back of the head..."

"Anything you can tell me about him that wasn't in the paper?"

He shook his head, then paused.

"I wouldn't swear to it, but seems like six months or thereabouts after he got sacked here, there was something in the paper about him getting arrested. It's like I said about him getting killed, when you see the name of someone you know and they're mixed up in something nasty, it kind of makes an impression."

"Do you happen to recall what he was arrested for?"

Hays tossed his rag from hand to hand and squinted in thought. "I think maybe stealing a car."

CHAPTER NINETEEN

The terrace had been empty when I pulled in behind it. Now Tinker and Arlene sat on the low wall around it. Their backs against large jardinieres of flowers, they faced each other with sections of newspaper in their laps.

"What are you doing here?" demanded Tinker, catching sight of me.

I had a feeling they'd noticed my car and were watching for me.

I sauntered toward them. "Oh, having a chat or two about an item in this morning's paper that you probably haven't seen since it doesn't have to do with fashion or gossip."

Arlene's chin jutted out. I'd hit a nerve. With unerring instinct, she grabbed the front section from the bottom of Tinker's pile and shook it at me.

"For your information I always read this section first, and I didn't see anything interesting." As she spoke, she unfolded it and scanned page one.

"Page three," I said. "Tiny little article, right hand side, near the bottom."

When she went rock still, I knew she'd spotted it.

"What?" Tinker swung her legs around and scooted to Arlene's side. "What is it?"

"That nasty Jimmy Delozier who worked here. Someone shot him. Killed him. Down by the river."

"Was he the one who was always sneaking around peeking in keyholes?"

"When you and Noah first were married. Yes. I don't know about keyholes, but he snooped."

"Well, good riddance. He gave me the creeps."

"Is this coffee hot?" Judith marched out from the hallway, stopping to touch the coffeepot on a table of midmorning fare that sat by the door. "Better than the tepid swill the maid brought anyway." She began to fill a clean cup as she continued to scatter her ire. "It's bad enough your father skipped breakfast. He at least—"

"He didn't skip breakfast. He had it with my mother."

Arlene's smile was swift, satisfied, and sharp.

Judith jammed the coffeepot down. "Well. Perhaps your mother could see to it that your father's coffee is hot when he wants a cup." Her eyes flicked over me and fixed on Tinker. "What was that about a shooting? Not around here I hope."

"Jimmy Delozier. He used to work here."

The secretary sucked in her breath. "He's the one," she said to me. "The one fired for stealing. Two people with ties to this family dead in less than a month. It's... it's..."

Abandoning the coffee she'd poured, she swerved back inside.

***

It was a toss up who would be first to get to the place where Delozier had lived when he worked for the Barretts, the cops or me. If the cops won, that was fine. What I'd learned from Hays and from the scene on the terrace had been worth the delay it caused me. Or so I told myself as I drove.

Hays's recollection that Delozier had been arrested for car theft was potentially the most valuable. It dovetailed nicely with a stolen car being used to run down Charlotte. It fit even better since he was familiar with the neighborhood, and even the house where she had been staying. Determining his motive would be the tricky part. From what I'd heard about him, I could see him committing murder for hire more easily than I could see one of the Barretts – or even Pammy Witherspoon – being a killer. I couldn't picture him being a customer at Mrs. Salmon's, but there was the bare chance he might have had some personal connection to Charlotte. That felt too close to tidy coincidence for my taste, but it would have to be checked. Hopefully, Lt. Freeze and his men would be the ones who did the checking.

Meanwhile, was there anything useful to know about the animosity between Arlene and Judith? I'd seen traces of it before, but there on the terrace it had been full blown. It seemed to have to do with Helen.

Judith's reaction when she heard the news about Delozier puzzled me. In most situations the secretary came across as calm and in control of things around her. Perhaps too much in control at times. Yet her jumble of words about two people with ties to the Barretts being dead had been almost hysterical.

***

If Jimmy Delozier had garnered any fans, I hadn't yet come across them. Neither the housekeeper nor the chauffeur fit that description, nor did Tinker or Arlene. Tinker's attitude had struck me as especially cold. But then I wasn't from a world where servants came and went. The world I came from was much more like the street of frame houses and small yards, some of them littered with kids' wagons, doll buggies or bicycles, where Delozier had lived when he worked for the Barretts.

"You're sure you're not a reporter?" his one-time landlady asked as she peered at my license.

"I'm sure." My arm was getting tired of holding it across the threshold.

The woman wore a blue and white checked apron

over her house dress, and a yellow bandana tied tightly around a head full of pincurls. She sighed with resignation.

"Well, I suppose it's my duty to help a detective. I read what happened to him in the paper this morning. Yes, he used to room here, but not for some time. Not since... you know. The trouble."

I played dumb. She peeked past me, left and right. Apparently, she didn't mind enlightening me, but she didn't want the neighbors to overhear.

"He went to prison, you know. For auto theft."

"Oh, yes."

"I wanted to put him out when he first got arrested. What decent person wants a roomer like that? But I have a cousin who used to work in a lawyer's office. She said I better let him stay until the trial was over – innocent until proven guilty and that – so that's what I did."

"I don't suppose you know where he'd been staying since he got back? Did he ask you to forward his mail, maybe?"

"Not only that, he showed up one day wanting to rent a room, bold as brass! I certainly wasn't going to have him after he'd been in prison. They learn things from each other, get worse than when they went in. When I told him no, I didn't have anything, he turned real sharp with me. Said I was turning my back on him because he'd made a mistake."

"But you don't know where he went after that."

"I know where he said he was staying. A week or so after that first time, he showed up all friendly like it never happened. It's what you said, he wanted me to forward his mail."

CHAPTER TWENTY

Finding Freeze took considerably less time and effort than getting the address of Delozier's former landlady. Brief as the item in the paper had been, it had mentioned that his body was found in a field near the fairgrounds. Since it also had referenced the river, I knew approximately where to look. I went south on Ludlow, then onto a couple of minor streets until I spotted a Dayton black-and-white plus two unmarked cars which I knew, even from a distance, belonged to detectives.

I found a place to pull off where no one could accuse me of interfering with traffic or blocking official vehicles. When I got out of the car, I felt the heat of the mid-day sun magnified by the wasteland around me. The imposing buildings of "The Cash," John Patterson's National Cash Register Company, held court not far away. Tossing my suit jacket into the car, I made my way toward the blocky shape that was Boike and the leaner one which was Freeze.

They turned as one at the sound of me.

Freeze scowled. "Somebody back at the office tell you where to find me?"

"I saved them the embarrassment of turning me down if I asked."

"What are you doing here?"

"I read about your new stiff in the paper this morning. I came to let you in on the daily special: Two homicides for the price of one."

Freeze lighted an Old Gold. He'd come up in the world. He snapped his thumb over not a match, but the flint of a metal lighter. I wondered if he'd acquired a girlfriend and she'd given it to him.

"What are you talking about?"

"Delozier used to work for the Barretts, the family that young woman killed in the hit-skip two weeks ago was supposed to marry into. He got fired for stealing some silver. Oh, yeah, and a few months back he finished serving a stretch for auto theft."

The detective swore for a full minute, after which he glowered at me. "So he worked for them. What makes you think there's a connection?"

"The fact he might have had a grudge. The fact he knew that neighborhood well enough to get away fast from a crime. The fact the car that killed Charlotte Littlefield was stolen."

"Yeah, yeah. Too much speculation for my taste."

"Too much coincidence for mine."

Boike, who was Freeze's right-hand man, had turned his blond head away to answer a question from one of the uniformed cops who were combing the area. He'd lost part of an ear in the war, but he was listening to the conversation.

Freeze puffed furiously until the uniformed cop moved on. He looked at the other detective. "What do you think, Boike?"

"While she lived with the Barretts, the hit-skip victim could have learned something Delozier was using to blackmail one of them."

"You figure she and Delozier might have known each other?"

"Possible."

"So he uses something she tells him—"

"Maybe that she just mentioned in passing."

"He uses that to squeeze money from someone in the Barrett household?"

"Something like that."

"And Delozier runs her down so she couldn't tell what she knew."

"It would explain a few things."

Their conversation had taken such an illogical twist I could scarcely speak.

"And you accuse me of jumping to conclusions? Where did you come up with blackmail? Or Charlotte being to blame for her own murder? Last time I talked to you, you wouldn't even consider her death might be a murder."

The two men looked at each other. Once upon a time, before the war, Freeze had come down heavily on any of his men who spoke unless he asked them something. Since Boike's return, Freeze had invited his input with some regularity. I watched an unspoken message pass between them.

"She might get more out of the Barretts than we can," Boike said.

Freeze dropped the butt of his cigarette under his heel and ground it out. He picked a lingering shred of tobacco from the tip of his tongue.

"We found more than two hundred in cash in an envelope taped behind Delozier's bureau," he said.

I gave a soft whistle. "That's a good wad of money."

"More than he made at his dishwashing job, that's for sure. Maybe enough to get him a .22 slug in the back of his skull."

"Not much if you're blackmailing somebody like the Barretts, though, I'd say."

Freeze grunted. "He could have spent the rest of it. Or he could have been getting monthly payments, smaller amounts that could be explained away as an ongoing expense."

Or it could have been a one-time payment to him for getting rid of Charlotte.

***

Delozier's murder, and the traipsing around I did afterward, threw a monkey wrench into my plan of attack for the day. If Arlene took off after lunch with her chum Pammy, as seemed to happen as often as not, I'd already missed her. A call to the Barrett home confirmed her absence.

"Is Tinker there?"

"I believe so. Let me get her."

"No, on second thought, just tell her that I may stop by later, but that she shouldn't change any plans because of me."

Was I one gracious gumshoe or what? I'd only wanted to learn who was keeping Arlene company. If it wasn't her sister-in-law, it was Pammy. Arlene didn't like being alone. That's precisely why I intended to get her that way, alone in a situation where she couldn't keep avoiding my questions.

Rather than risk putting Pammy on guard with a phone call, even one where I hung up without saying a word, I drove to her apartment house. Her car was in back. Once I'd established that, I pulled my DeSoto back into the street and did a U-turn into a spot at the curb which would give me a fine view of Pammy's car leaving her building's parking lot.

Sitting in my car for hours on end and watching for someone or some activity was the worst of the chores required of a private eye, as far as I was concerned. What I had in mind for these two girls who'd come to irritate like thorns beneath my skin promised at least a dab of fun, though. Ignoring the nap of my upholstery, which prickled my back in warm weather, I settled in to wait and to think about what I'd learned from Freeze and Boike.

Only one set of tire tracks had been visible when the police arrived. Either Delozier had walked to the site or he had come with his killer. However he arrived, he left with a hole from a .22 in the back of his skull. They'd recovered the bullet, which would help if they ever found a gun to match it to. The physical description Freeze gave me, along with the fact that the only bullet hole in Delozier was the one in his head, cemented the fact he wasn't the one who attacked me in Pammy's parking lot.

So far, the detectives didn't know much about the dead man's habits, or they weren't telling me. Freeze seemed interested in the address I had given him for the place Delozier lived before going to prison.

"We'll talk to some of the staff at the Barrett place, routine questions," Freese said. "At this point, we won't suggest any connection between this and the death of the Littlefield woman. We'll count on you to let us know if you pick up on something."

His agreeable tone didn't fool me. He was counting on my having better rapport with them than he and his men were likely to establish. In short, he needed me on this, so he'd coughed up more information than he ordinarily would. I didn't delude myself such cooperation would last.

The appearance of Pammy's car pulling onto the street saved me from further ruminations. I recognized Arlene's blond head in the passenger seat. Starting my engine, I tagged along behind them.

It took about three blocks before they realized I was there. I knew it had happened when Arlene jerked around to get a better look. I waved and smiled, knowing she probably couldn't see. Unlike an ordinary tail where I didn't want to be spotted, I didn't bother to keep even one car between us.

Pammy stomped on the gas, then slowed as she decided not to speed. Possibly she'd had a few too many tickets already. She was headed north for the center of town. Suddenly she swerved and turned, cutting in front of a car whose driver leaned on the horn. I turned more sedately a block later. And caught up with her as she headed north again on a parallel street. She tried a U-turn. I did the same. She zigged and zagged and went across the river.

Finally, she pulled to the curb. Red blotched her cheeks as she got out and stood with her fists on her hips. The color did nothing to improve her looks.

"I'm nearly out of gas. Why are you following me?" The society girl looked ready to sock me harder than the fellow who'd jumped me in the parking lot. Arlene exited the car more slowly than her friend as I strolled up to join them. We were standing in front of a vacuum cleaner repair place that didn't appear to be doing a very brisk business.

"I thought it might be fun to hear the fairytales you'd spin me about where you were last night when Jimmy Delozier was murdered."

Pammy looked more angry than anything else. "What's she talking about?" she demanded, whirling on Arlene.

"He-he used to work for us. Someone shot him last night."

"Well, I never heard of him, so don't ask me."

"See, the way I figure it, the two of you have been lying about where you were when Charlotte was killed because you were waiting for Delozier to report it was done and collect his payment. Did you pay him with cash, or with fun in the bedroom?"

"That's disgusting!" Arlene's expression matched her words. "He was — he was pimply and nasty."

"But you were afraid he'd blab, so last night you got rid of him."

I kept my eyes fixed on Pammy's. She hadn't yet asked why I thought she'd want Charlotte dead.

"I'm going to ruin you," she said instead.

"I don't suppose you happen to have a gun."

"Yeah, several. Just like my grandpop has several lawyers."

Arlene was chewing her lip and looking from one of

us to the other. "Come on, Pammy. I need to get home and you have to—"

"Shut up, you big baby." She gave Arlene a shove and started around to the driver's side. "I don't have time to take you home to Mommy. Get a trolley."

Slinging herself behind the wheel, she took off with a squeal of tires.

CHAPTER TWENTY-ONE

Arlene stared after her for several seconds. She had forgotten my presence.

"Bitch," she said under her breath.

"An accurate description."

"Just because she's probably never ridden a trolley in her life she doesn't think I can, or will." She turned away.

"Wait," I said. "I've got something to do down your way. I can drop you off at your house."

"While you give me the third degree again?" Arlene arched an eyebrow but without hostility. Somewhere in that last angry exchange she had stepped into the sensibility of a twenty-three-year-old in a family with no shortage of either brains or common sense.

"Hard to say. Habits die hard."

She watched me get into the car and then got in herself. Neither of us spoke until we crossed the river back into downtown.

"We were at a burlesque theater. Pammy thought she might get a job there. To pay off her debt. She wanted to see what they did first, and I went with her."

I burst out laughing.

"It's true. And yes, I've heard that story about crying wolf."

"I believe you."

"It's on East Second and the name's the Harem and it's kind of a dump. Why are you still laughing?"

"Because there's absolutely nothing wrong with going to a burlesque. You're both plenty old enough." I struggled to get my snickers under control.

"Nothing wrong with it! My mother would be so disappointed in me if she knew! Dad would hit the ceiling. Have you ever been to a place like that?"

From the side of my eye, I could see she was red with embarrassment.

"Sure, a couple of times. They have good comics on the bills sometimes and some of the dance numbers are pretty showy. From the address of this one though, it's not exactly the cream of the crop."

"No." Arlene looked down at her hands. "They had a stripper. And some of the men in the audience..." She shuddered.

"I take it Pammy changed her mind about working there?"

She shook her head. "No. I couldn't believe it. Afterward she went to the ticket seller and said she was interested in working there and could she talk to the manager. He just about fell over himself offering her a job in the chorus. I guess she'd had three or four years of dance while she was in school. That's what families like ours do with their girl children, send them to dance lessons, deportment lessons. Anyway, that's where she was supposed to go after she took me home. They're going to get her costume fitted."

At Court Street I cut over to Main. "Why is Pammy in debt?"

"Gambling. This guy she was dating went to poker games. The stakes were pretty high. She tried it too – probably because it looked exciting. At first she won, but then she didn't. Now she owes a lot. More than she can sweettalk out of her gramps."

We drove for a minute.

"What about you? Do you go to the games? Do you owe money too?"

"Gamble? Do you think I'm stupid?"

It was my turn to arch of brow and her turn to chuckle, albeit after a pause and weakly. Her fingertip traced the metal strip that trimmed the side window well. "I don't know what I ever saw in her. I wish I'd stayed at school. But Mother was in the hospital and I was scared I wouldn't see her again and the only class I really liked was chemistry."

"I noticed the chemistry book when I came to your room. Is that the one you used?"

"Are you kidding? No, it was one of Dad's, but I couldn't even understand a third of it."

"Your dad studied chemistry?"

"It's what he does, chemistry. What the company does, sort of. It's why he has the lab in back. I guess my grandpa used it, but I don't remember him much, and Dad never used it before. He did mostly business things in the office downtown. That's right next door to the building with the main laboratories. But when the war started and the government asked him to work on some project, he started using this one so he could stay near to Mother. He and Mr. McDowell use it mostly for checking results, I think. The rest of the team work at the one downtown."

We were now within a couple of blocks of her house. My time for raising another subject was short. "The university offers some night courses. They might have one or two in chemistry. But listen, Arlene, there's something I need to tell you before we get to your house, and I don't want you playing games when I do. Once the police find out Jimmy Delozier used to work for your family, which they will, they'll show up asking questions. Most likely they'll only talk to the staff, but they may want to talk to the family too. If they do, what are you prepared to tell them about where you were last night?"

"At home. Playing canasta with Jack until, I don't know, midnight or so."

"Any witnesses?"

"Who aren't part of the family or someone who works for us, you mean?"

There was more than a little cynicism to the new Arlene. I still liked her better than the old model. I hoped she didn't fall under Pammy's spell again. "Yes, that's exactly what I mean."

She frowned in thought. "A man from the downtown lab brought something for Dad sometime after eleven. I answered the front door. They lock the door in the lab here at ten and Dad had sent Mr. McDowell home and told Griggs to go on to bed. Since Jack and I were in the living room anyway, we said we'd let the man in. I don't know his name."

The driveway to her house was just ahead. I slowed. "Okay if I drop you here at the bottom?" I asked. I had used as much gas following Pammy as she had eluding me.

Arlene nodded. We came to a stop and she opened the door.

"Hey," I said when she got out. "What have you got against Judith?"

She snorted. "My mother's frail. Judith orders Griggs and the others around like she runs the house as well as the office. She has the bedroom next to my father's. You figure it out."

CHAPTER TWENTY-TWO

Get Arlene on her own and she was halfway decent, I reflected as I drove back toward town. She was looking less and less like a murder suspect. Pammy, on the other hand, revealed more viciousness with every encounter.

I was so absorbed in my thoughts that I didn't notice the plump little figure trudging along and making swipes at her eyes until I was past her. It was Janine, the upstairs maid who had seemed to know more than she told me about the state Charlotte left her room in. Her head was down. She took another swipe at her eyes.

Deciding quickly, I pulled to the curb and walked back to meet her. "Hey, Janine. What's wrong?"

"Nothing. Just catching my bus home."

A block ahead was a bus stop, the same one Charlotte had been headed for, most likely.

"Kind of early isn't it?"

Her lip trembled. "Mrs. Randall sent me home and docked me a whole day's pay for dropping a cup."

"Gee, that's awfully strict," I sympathized. "Let me

give you a ride since I'm headed that way. It'll save you bus fare, at least."

She started to refuse but couldn't. "Okay. Thanks."

We rode in silence for a few minutes.

"You know what cheers me up when I'm having a rough day?" I said. "Pie. I'll bet a piece of pie would make you feel better. Let me buy you a piece. There's a place that makes good ones up ahead."

Desire flooded her mouth. I could hear her swallow.

"I'd better not. Mama says I eat too many sweets."

"Mama won't be with us, will she?"

A tiny giggle escaped her. Maggie Sullivan, handmaiden to the Devil.

The place we went to did serve excellent pie. I'd forgotten it was lunchtime. The tiny table we managed to get in a corner had remained vacant thanks to a seriously wobbly leg. While we worked on our respective treats, I went on about how hard it must be working in a house with so many people to please.

"If one of them isn't out of sorts, I'll bet Mrs. Randall is," I said.

The maid rolled her eyes. "I don't think anything ever satisfies Mrs. Randall. Ever." She stabbed at her pie.

I rested my chin on my hand. "That powder you mentioned that Miss Littlefield dumped in the trash —

I've been thinking about it. I'll bet it was really nice powder. Expensive, I mean. Why would anybody throw it out?"

Janine's fork slowed. Her eyes flicked from her plate to me. "You won't tell on me? I didn't do anything wrong, but Mrs. Randall..."

"Our secret." I crossed my heart.

"I saw it there, thrown out, with the lid off and part of it spilled, and I-I thought like you did. That it must be nice. So I thought, why not take it? Since she'd thrown it away. But when I went to take it out of the wastebasket, I saw these pieces of broken glass mixed in with it. One so long and sharp it could put your eye out if it popped off the powder puff. She must have dropped a glass or something."

"Yeah."

I didn't believe it for a minute. Taking a big bite of pie in the name of innocence, I played a hunch. "Tell me about the mouse, or rat, whichever it was."

"A mouse. Just a little bitty gray mouse." She indicated with her fingers.

"What about it?"

She looked at me stupidly. "It was caught. In a mousetrap. It was dead."

"Was it on her bed? Her pillow?"

"No, it was there on her dressing table. The day before I heard Mrs. Randall say someone upstairs complained about seeing a mouse. She told Patsy –

that's one of the other maids – to put out poison. I guess maybe Miss Littlefield didn't know about that and put a trap out."

"A dressing table's kind of a strange place to set a mousetrap, don't you think?"

"I don't know. Maybe she just wanted to make sure we saw it when we cleaned up."

Not a girl fleeing for her life, I thought. Someone had put it there. It was a threat, and a warning.

***

What was the proper attire for paying a visit to the management of a burlesque theater? That was the decision facing me Saturday morning. Unlike Pammy, I wanted to make it crystal clear that I wasn't there to apply for a job, so trousers seemed wise. I put on the pair I'd worn the previous day; nice fawn linen with a wide waist band. Adding a white blouse with Peter Pan collar and a short nutmeg flecked tan jacket. I was set to take on the world – or at least the management of the Harem burlesque.

It was in a neighborhood that had more than its share of winos and hookers at night. By day it managed to just pass as decent. When I got there at ten in the morning, the surrounding streets were still sleepy. Since such establishments ran shows in the daytime as well as night, a large sign with the word

CLOSED filled the front window. To keep eager beavers at bay. Smaller letters below said the first show started at noon. I went around to the side door, which as I had expected, was propped partway open.

Stepping inside I heard the sound of a piano more interested in reinforcing the beat of a piece than of musicality. I could see the steps leading up to the side of the stage but not the dancers thumping along as they practiced some routine.

"Can I help you?" demanded a gruff looking guy who looked set to throw me out. He could probably do it. He was shorter than I was but made up for it by being several times wider, some of it muscle.

"Yeah, you can let me speak to whoever's in charge here." I gave him a card.

It didn't make him look any friendlier as he scowled, looked me up and down a couple of times, and stalked away. With a smile for a stagehand who was warily watching me, I managed a few steps to the side. From there I could see the far end of the stage and occasionally a glimpse of dancers. I couldn't tell if Pammy was among them.

My greeting committee of one returned, accompanied by a man with slicked back hair and a checkered suit that hurt my eyes. He inventoried my physical assets before he reached me.

"What's the problem?"

"No problem." I wasted one of my better smiles on

him. "I just want to ask a few questions." I held out my hand. "Maggie Sullivan."

The action caught him off guard enough that he shook it.

"And you are…?" I prompted.

"Terry. Terry Crocker. What kind of questions?"

"I want to know if a couple of girls came here and talk to you recently." From my handbag I removed the photo of Arlene and Pammy that I'd shown at the USO club. "These two."

One brief glance and he thrust it back at me. "Yeah, they came here. I hired one of them. Anything else? We open in a couple of hours and I've got lots to do."

"Just tell me the date you hired her, and I'll be out of your hair."

According to Arlene, somebody at the burlesque had hired Pammy on the day they went there. Establish when Pammy had signed, and I would have proven Arlene's whereabouts at the time of Charlotte's murder.

"You want to know that, ask her. She was old enough. I hired her. It's a free country. So unless you've got a warrant, I don't see why I should tell you anything else."

Placing a fingertip on the side of my chin I cocked my head at Terry. "Maybe because her grandfather wouldn't be thrilled about her working in a place like this. And because he has money enough to buy Fort Knox and even more lawyers. Or don't you keep records?"

He glowered. "Pick up the pace. It's not a funeral march," he bellowed at a woman watching the dancers from a seat in the darkened audience. "Checking the records will take a minute. They're in the office," he said to me.

"Lead the way."

He opened his mouth as though to argue, then closed it again. I followed him up a set of stairs at one side of the stage. In a room cluttered with framed posters of singers, standup comics, and a few very scantily clad dancers, he sat down behind a surprisingly tidy desk. Opening a drawer, he took out a folder and shuffled through papers until he found the one he was hunting.

"Hired her on the fourth. She gave her name as Pamela Witherspoon. If that's not right, that's your concern, not mine."

"That's her name all right," I said with a grin. "What about a man named Jimmy Delozier? What do you know about him?"

CHAPTER TWENTY-THREE

"Have you ever had any dealings with a man named Delozier?" I asked Mrs. Salmon.

I posed the question from the comfort of my office. Why waste gas on a trip to her place to ask her in person when I could do it over the phone? My lunch was spread out on my desk. I sat enjoying stewed apples, a bread-and-butter sandwich, a boiled egg, and a handful of watercress.

"If so it's been so long ago I don't remember."

"This would have been the past six years, maybe the last four. He probably wasn't a customer. Someone who did odd jobs, yard work, delivery man, maybe."

"You think he could be connected to what happened to Charlotte?"

I swallowed a bit of egg with some cress tucked around it. "I don't know. He used to work for the Barretts. I'd like to know if he ever crossed paths with her."

"I'll ask the girls. Maybe one of them's heard of him." There was curiosity in her voice.

We said the things that people say to end the

conversation. After that I let myself have a brief wallow in irritation over the time I'd spent on Pammy and Arlene only to have it lead to a dead end. I was glad Arlene was in the clear, though.

Who did that leave, and what was the motive? There was blackmail, if I bought the theory Boike had suggested, but I didn't. Even if Charlotte had known Delozier, say in the past, the chances that she would encounter him in the short time she'd lived with the Barretts were simply too small. Certainly, she wouldn't have spent enough time with him to tell him anything worthy of blackmail.

Except there was one opportunity for her to run into him. Her daily walk.

"Nope," I said to the dead plant that had long held court from a corner next to my window. "Everything I've heard about her argues that she wouldn't tell him something deliberately. Why would he even be walking where she could run into him unless he was headed to the Barrett place to ask for work? He'd already tried that when he first got out of the pen and Hays turned him down – in spades, to hear his telling."

The phone rang.

"How dare you sic the police on us again!" demanded a voice on the other end.

"I beg your pardon?"

"They almost breeched the security of a defense project!"

"Is this Judith? Miss Todd?"

My caller banged her phone down in reply.

I finished my stewed apples.

Yesterday Freeze had indicated the men he sent to the Barrett place would ask only cursory questions of family members, focusing instead on the household staff with whom Delozier might have interacted. I was sure my caller had been Barrett's secretary, and she had sounded properly agitated. Had something turned up in Freeze's investigation that caused him to change his plan? Curious, I headed over to see what had happened. I wanted to ask Jack something anyway.

***

It occurred to me that it might be wise for me to go in the back way, meaning the side door at the rear of the house. If the police had created as much of a dither as Judith had indicated, Griggs might be under orders to turn me away from the front. While I had no qualms about dealing with a recalcitrant butler, the fewer feathers I ruffled, the sooner I'd get to the truth about Charlotte Littlefield's murder. I recalled what Arlene had said about Judith trying to run the household the same way she ran Simon's office.

The same maid who'd let me in the last time I used the rear entrance answered my knock again.

"Mrs. Randall's not going to like it if you take time talking to people again," she said when she saw me. "The police were here asking questions and we're all behind."

"I just wanted to measure how long it takes to walk from this door to the living room," I said with what I hoped was detective-like mystery.

"Oh. Okay. Go on then." She scurried away.

Freed of the need to pretend, I started for the living room and Jack's small office nearby.

"Miss Sullivan."

Simon Barrett called to me through the open door to the terrace, where he stood with a glass of milk in his hand. I stepped out to join him. If he was upset the police had been there, he didn't show it. He gave a friendly smile. "Are your inquiries yielding anything?"

"Not much, I'm afraid. Judith called and said the police were disrupting things. I thought I should come and see."

He made a dismissive gesture with the milk. "I'd hardly call it a disruption. I hope you didn't come here just for that."

"I also need a word with Jack."

"Ah. He and Arlene went over to the university. I nearly choked on my chicken last night when she asked whether she might be able to take some chemistry courses there without enrolling full time."

He threw me an amused glance. "Something she said made me think you might have given her the idea, in which case you deserve a gold star. Jack has a friend on the faculty there, so he went to make introductions."

As he talked, Simon Barrett raised his white beard to the sky and breathed deeply as if savoring these moments outdoors and away from his work. I felt a twinge of guilt at intruding on the solitude he might have enjoyed. The blue canvas of the umbrellas fluttered in a gentle breeze. A small stack of lunch dishes not yet cleared away bore witness to the fact the household staff were behind in their duties.

Before I could move on and leave him in peace, angry footsteps clicked over the threshold.

"How dare you tell the police that Jimmy Delozier had worked here!" Judith demanded. "Dragging this family into something sordid and totally unrelated to it, as if they haven't been through enough already!"

"Did they say I told them about Delozier being employed here?"

Unaccustomed to being challenged, Judith drew herself up. "Well, no."

"Give the police some credit for being intelligent, Judith. They look for the same sort of links I do, and one of the first things I'd do would be talk to people where a victim had worked."

Her lips thinned with displeasure. "Whether you

told them or not, your digging into Miss Littlefield's death brought us to their attention."

There was absolutely no logic for her conclusion.

"Do you realize they nearly breeched security on a highly sensitive government project?" she continued.

"Judith." Simon Barrett put his hand on her shoulder and gave it a small, reassuring shake. "You're working yourself up over nothing. As soon as I came to the door of the lab and showed our certification, they were quite accommodating. Five minutes of very polite questions and they were done. I'm sorry if they interfered with your work, but I really think Griggs and the rest of the household staff got the worst of it."

For the second time, her lips tightened. "Of course." She shot me a hostile look.

Giving her shoulder a final pat, Simon turned and set the glass he'd been drinking from on the side table.

"I'd have been more than happy to bring you some milk." Judith forced a smile.

"I know. I like a breath of fresh air now and then. Was there anything you wanted?"

"Just to know where you were in case there was a phone call."

"Not up to any mischief, I assure you. I'll be back in a minute."

The dismissal was unmistakable. Her body stiffened. With a small nod, she turned and left.

Simon ambled toward the terrace wall, flexing his arms to stretch them.

"Wonderful woman, Judith, but she does fuss at times. I'm afraid the house is rather empty just now, Miss Sullivan. Helen and her nurse are off at a doctor's appointment. Jack and Arlene are away, as I mentioned. Noah's back with us..."

"Who's that?" I interrupted. A man in coveralls was crawling along in the bushes on the other side of the back door. Had the cops turned up something that warranted going over the area outside the house with a fine-toothed comb?

"Ah. That's Mr. Fenton, the gardener. He used to be here every day, but we lost the groundskeeper at the building downtown, so he divides his time between the two places. Crochety old fellow, but second to none in his work."

"Was he here the day Charlotte was killed?"

Simon thought a moment. "I couldn't say."

I excused myself. Whether or not Fenton had been here that day, he'd surely met her a time or two while she lived here. By the sounds of it, he'd probably worked for the Barretts long enough to remember Jimmy Delozier too. Fenton worked outside, where Delozier had often worked, and where he would see things those inside didn't. When I located him, he was just around the corner from the side door, on his knees and staring mournfully at the back wall of the house.

"Mr. Fenton? My name's Maggie Sullivan. Jack Barrett hired me to look into the accident that killed Miss Littlefield. I'm a private detective."

"Oh yes?" The shock of hair flopping onto his lined, weathered face seemed out of place, a piece of his youth that hadn't caught up with the rest of him. He gestured with the clippers in his hand. "Just look at that. That's what happens when ivy that used to get clipped every week only gets it once a month."

Leaning forward, he clipped off a small tendril. Small sounds of disapproval escaped him.

"I expect you talked to her a few times."

"The girl Mr. Jack was going to marry? Oh yes. Nice girl. Followed me around twice, maybe three times, all interested in what kind of plants I was working on, and what I was doing to them."

He broke off to lean forward and scowl. "Cigarette butt," he muttered. He whisked it out with the tip of his fingers. "Stuffed back here when there's a trash can two steps away. If there's half a dozen like I found last week, I'll just have to speak up."

"Mr. Fenton..."

He went nose-to-nose with the ivy and made two snips as precisely as a doctor stitches a wound.

"Oh yes, the girl who was killed. Real sweet she was. Once when I was planting bulbs, she asked if she could plant some. I told her she'd better change out of her nice dress first, and she did. She got down and dug just like I showed her, and put half a dozen bulbs in the ground. You'd have thought I'd given her a million dollars."

"Were you here the day she was killed?"

"No. Sad. She might have made a gardener."

Threading callused fingers through the ivy vines, he plucked out his two latest clippings and added them to the pile beside him.

"People don't understand how it sets plants back when you don't do right by them. Makes them lag. And look at this, stuffed down just because somebody wanted it out of their way. Faded as it is, it's been here almost since the last time I did the ivy, too."

According to what he'd said earlier, that had been a month ago. Jimmy Delozier had still been alive. Charlotte Littlefield had still been alive.

The object that had drawn the gardener's ire was a matchbook. Once upon a time its cover had been red. It had faded to an indeterminate pinkish beige. Retrieving it from the pile of Fenton's discards, I held it up to my eyes in hopes of making out an image or the name of a business.

Nothing. But only at first glance. By tilting it this way and that and filling in a letter or two, I had a name, then, at the bottom edge where it wasn't as faded, an address.

Judging by that address, it wasn't a place the Barretts would patronize. But Jimmy Delozier might.

CHAPTER TWENTY-FOUR

The matchbook was from a place called The Little Red Tavern. What the name lacked in originality, the building itself attempted to compensate for with two almost life size cancan dancers painted on the front. Otherwise, it was small, and as ruby hued as if a kid with a starter's box of crayons had colored it. It was out on East First in a working class neighborhood with one toe over the line towards being tough.

As I came up the street, I spotted the car Freeze drove parked at the curb near the tavern entrance. A white-on-black squad car was parked in front of his. The words I'd so recently spouted to Judith about the cops being smarter than she gave them credit for came back to haunt me. One of the first things detectives wanted to learn in a homicide was what bars or clubs the victim had frequented. I wondered how they'd managed to do it so quickly.

The police presence meant I wouldn't be welcome. On the bright side, it confirmed my hunch that Delozier was the one who had stuffed his empty matchbook into the ivy. The gardener who tended the ivy was more vigilant about his little green charges than most mothers were about their toddlers. If he said the matchbook hadn't been there a month ago, I had no doubt that sometime in the last month Jimmy Delozier had stood there in that hidden spot long enough to light a cigarette and discard a matchbook.

As far as I was concerned, the matchbook went a long way toward proving some link between Charlotte's death and Jimmy Delozier. For the moment I didn't want to explore the implications of that. And since I couldn't talk to anyone at the Little Red Tavern just now, I had time to call Mrs. Salmon before she became unavailable for the rest of the day.

***

"I didn't find any mention of a Delozier in my records, either as an employee or a customer," she reported. "I went back eight years."

"What about the girls who work there? Have you had a chance to talk to them yet?"

"Each one, individually. Nobody had even heard the name before, let alone Charlotte mentioning it. There's one girl she was particularly close to—"

"Audrey?"

"Yes. She told me that once when the two of them were in a cab, going to get their hair done, she thinks, the cab had to wait while a man with a dolly wheeled a piece of equipment down the ramp of a delivery van and into a store. Audrey said she pressed her face right up against the window watching. Charlotte told her the man looked exactly like someone she'd gone to school with."

"Could it have been?"

"Audrey asked. Charlotte said no, the boy she knew had drowned."

I was silent. Sometimes people thought to be drowned turned up alive months, or even years, later.

"Any chance Audrey recalls what he looked like?"

Mrs. Salmon chuckled. "I thought you might ask that. Big, she said, big and fit. Blond. She told me he looked like a Swede. Does that sound like the fellow you're hunting?"

"I don't need to hunt; he's in the morgue. But no, there's not a shred of similarity. People acquainted with Jimmy Delozier have described him as 'a skinny little weasel' and 'a sewer rat.' He had dark hair. He used to work for the Barretts until they fired him. Two nights ago, he turned up dead with a bullet in the back of his head. That's why I was curious."

This time it was Mrs. Salmon who didn't speak.

"If you learn anything or need anything, let me know, will you?" she said at last, but I wasn't listening. Mick Connelly, who had pursued me quietly and patiently for years while I'd resisted out of fear of failure and of being tied down, had just walked into my office.

***

"I knocked," he said in apology.

"I guess it didn't register."

"I didn't hear you talking—"

"It's okay."

He was wearing off-duty clothes, a brown jacket open over his shirt. It brought out the brown in his brindled but largely brick-colored hair.

"You making any progress with that hit-skip for the high society clients?"

"I'm not sure." I leaned forward. "Are you here to tell me it's been kicked to homicide?"

"Not so far as I know. I have the day off. Which is why I'm here." He stuffed his hands in his pockets. "Seamus offered to stay with the kids if I wanted to have an evening out on my own. Have a sandwich and go to a movie, he said. I thought I'd rather take you to dinner. If you were interested."

The old terror rose in my throat. I fought it.

"As friends, if that's how you want it," he added.

I nodded. "For now anyway. Okay. Yes. Having a good talk with you over dinner sounds grand. I've... missed that."

He smiled, not so much with his mouth as with a crinkling at the corners of his steel blue eyes.

"I may embarrass us both by reaching across the table and cutting up your meat."

I laughed.

***

We went to a place on East Fifth where we'd often gone in years past. It was brick walled and unpretentious with a large dining room adjacent to the bar. I wore a dress I'd bought before the war and hadn't had many chances to wear, since it was too pretty for work. The navy blue background was patterned with sprays of flowers in pastel blue, pink and white. It had cuffs above the elbow and swung around me when I walked.

Connelly had on a single-breasted tweed jacket that picked up the gray in his trousers. He had the waist for single breasted.

"To the future," he said lifting his glass of whiskey.

I touched it with the rim of my martini.

"It looks like there might really be one, with the Nazis being routed from city after city. Have you heard anything from your family?"

His hard face softened, as it always did at mention of his mother and siblings in Ireland. Supposedly Eire was neutral, but the Germans kept such a close watch on it that communication with Allied countries was difficult.

"I've a young cousin works for the telegraph. The Germans must not be watching as close, at least in little market towns like his, for he sent me a telegram yesterday, bold as brass. Said Ma and the rest are all fine. 'Letters soon,' it said, too, which I take to mean things are loosening up."

"That's good to hear."

"Yeah, it is. So. Are you glad you bought a house?"

The subject surprised me as much as the change of direction.

"Yeah. Even with paying taxes and utilities I save a bit over what I paid at Mrs. Z's. More than that, though, I like having a place of my own. Even with having to clean, and a broken water pipe and such."

He nodded.

"I'm thinking of buying one. I've talked to the bank and they're willing to lend me the money. The thing is, Kathleen just about drained our savings, so I might be going out on a limb."

I straightened my cutlery, hoping he wouldn't notice my anger. He did.

"Did I say something wrong? Would you rather I not mention her?"

I shook my head. "It has nothing to do with Kathleen. I was thinking how bank after bank turned me down for a mortgage because I wasn't a man. Because I didn't have a husband. It was only when Seamus put in nearly his whole savings that it happened."

Connelly leaned across the table, ducking his head so I couldn't avoid his eyes. "And never was a man happier over a deal, Maggie. He never thought he'd have a proper home again, he told me, and now he does. And he's like a kid over that yard and his garden."

My moment of sourness receded. "Yeah, he is. And I'm glad for you, Mick. Honestly. You deserve a break."

"The thing is, Maggie, I don't know if I'll ever get a chance like this again."

Over dinner he told me about it. Another cop he was friends with had inherited his family home when his mother died. The cop was a bachelor, content with his small apartment, and had a sister who was feeble-minded and needed round-the-clock minding. If he sold the house, he could use the proceeds to pay for her care in a good institution.

"What do the kids think?" I asked as we lingered over coffee cups long grown empty. Somewhere at the end of the meal, Connelly had stretched his legs out under the table. I hadn't objected to the familiar feel of them against mine.

"I haven't mentioned it to them yet. Didn't want to get them excited unless I made a decision."

"Well, you do have that sergeant's pay now," I teased.

He chuckled. "And being diligent in my new duties, I checked in with the relief sergeant this afternoon to see if there was anything new I should be prepared for when I go in tomorrow. He said Lieutenant

Freeze had requested the file on that hit-skip you asked about last week. So there's your sweet at the end of the meal. He may be looking at it as a homicide."

"Kicking and screaming all the way," I said.

We rose as one. As we headed out into the April evening, I sketched in the basics of Delozier's connection to the Barretts, and Freeze's theory that any link between Delozier's death and Charlotte's would indicate blackmail.

"Look on the bright side," said Connelly. "If he looks into that angle, you don't have to. It keeps him out of your hair, and you benefit if he learns something."

"Except I think he's wrong on the blackmail angle. I think someone hired him to kill Charlotte and then killed him to shut him up. Which means I'm back to hunting a motive in a small group of people with more cross-currents rippling through them than the Great Miami."

"What if you start at the other end instead?" Connelly took my elbow to help me into the car. "Who of the people you're looking into has access to a car and was out the night this Delozier was murdered?"

CHAPTER TWENTY-FIVE

On Monday I gave Freeze an hour to share what he'd learned at the Little Red Tavern as a token of his gratitude over my tip about Delozier's past employment at the Barretts. When he didn't, I went to his office to help him get over his shyness.

"What did you find out at the Little Red Tavern?" I asked, sinking onto a chair in front of his desk.

He'd already been out somewhere. While shrugging out of his jacket, on the verge of sitting, he was looking at messages that had accumulated in his absence. His head snapped up to look at me.

"How did you find out about the place and what do you know that you haven't been telling me?"

"By relentless detective work which didn't involve being told by anyone at the Barretts, in case you're wondering. Who told you?"

"I have sources. I repeat, what do you know about Delozier going there?"

"Nothing. You were already there when I drove up. I didn't think you'd appreciate my presence. The place is closed Sunday and Monday, so here I am waiting to be filled in."

Freeze snorted.

"You take a lot for granted. No one knew him by name; we had to show his picture. The owners and some of the regulars remember seeing him there a couple of times a week, but never with anyone in particular. Not with anyone, period, generally. More than a couple called him cocky or a smart Alec. Not a popular guy." He leaned back and started an Old Gold. "So," he said, blowing smoke out, "which of the Barrett clan is most likely to have done something they could be blackmailed over?"

I gave it honest thought. Freeze watched me closely.

"The brother maybe. Noah." All I really had to go on was his hostile attitude. "Or possibly his wife Tinker. She's the only one who admits to not liking Charlotte." There was also the matter of her cold reaction to Delozier's murder. "Does this mean you've decided Charlotte Littlefield's death was a homicide?"

"Yeah, probably. Now scram. Every time you walk in you complicate my life."

"I like to think I add zest." I bounced to my feet.

"So does horseradish," said Freeze, "but it gives me gas."

***

Having someone come up with a better idea than mine was nearly as unpalatable to me as it was to Freeze. The exception was Mick Connelly. I had always found batting things back and forth with him useful. The idea he'd tossed out about working backward from who had access to a car the night Delozier was murdered made sense. It gave me two reasons for paying a call on the Barretts.

To my surprise, the door to Jack's office which usually stood open was closed when I got there. Through it I heard the voices of two other men.

"Is Jack likely to be very long, do you think?" I asked Griggs. "I have a quick question." Namely whether Charlotte had ever mentioned the Little Red Tavern.

"At least an hour I should think," said the butler. "He's getting the monthly reports and the men just arrived."

Arlene was out, as was Tinker. Miss Archer, he thought, was with Mrs. Barrett. Mr. Barrett and Mr. McDowell were in a meeting at the downtown offices.

Talking to the household staff was also on my agenda, so I just moved it to the top. My brief chats failed to turn up anyone who so much as admitted to recognizing the name of the place from the matchbook cover.

"A girl I know wants me to meet her there so she

can introduce me to her cousin," I explained once I'd asked a few unimportant cover questions. "I'd like to make sure it isn't a dive, you know?"

Janine and another maid responded to the question about the Little Red Tavern with fits of giggles. A third looked as though I had asked her to jump off a bridge and told me she was a Baptist – whatever that meant. The others simply said no.

I went out the side door and stood for a minute, confirming that I couldn't see the spot where the matchbook had been tucked in the ivy. Then I made my way to the garage to talk to Hays. The chauffeur frowned for a decent interval before saying he thought he'd heard the name somewhere but wasn't sure and couldn't recall any details.

Back in the house I made my way to the terrace and checked from various spots to determine if I could see the spot where Delozier and someone else had stood talking long enough for one of them to finish a cigarette and stuff a used matchbook into the ivy rather than walk a few steps to the trashcan. I couldn't.

Since the housekeeper didn't read tawdry headlines, I spared my ears the abuse they would get if I asked her about a tavern. Instead, I looked for Griggs and found him in the front hall where he was supervising a young male underling as he set an enormous vase of florist flowers on a table and carefully lifted the one it was replacing.

"May I help you with anything, Miss?" he asked.

Behind the mostly closed door to Jack's office, men were still talking.

"A couple of questions if you have time."

"Of course."

"What can you tell me about a place called the Little Red Tavern? Have any of the staff ever mentioned it?"

The butler's nostrils thinned. "I don't believe so, but I wouldn't have paid much attention, I'm afraid. I enjoy a nice cocktail now and again, but only in my apartment or in a restaurant prior to dinner."

Behind us the voices from the makeshift office crescendoed as the door opened wide and Jack stepped out with his cane.

"Could we have coffee, please, Griggs?" Noting my presence, he gave a vague nod and was gone again as quickly as he had appeared.

"Your other question?" Griggs said to me, eager to fetch the requested coffee.

"The family car, the one that's shared. Is there a system for determining who uses it when?"

"I'll explain that if you'll see these go with the outgoing mail," said another voice.

It was Judith, coming from the wing that housed Simon Barrett's offices and laboratory. She handed Griggs a stack of letters. He hurried off and she gave me an indulgent smile.

"Daytime, the car is reserved for Helen's needs – getting her to doctor's appointments, picking up prescriptions and medical items she might need – and for office errands. Evenings it's whoever wants it, if it's not already spoken for. Why?"

"Just curious. Is there some sort of list of who's using it, or scheduled to use it?"

"Yes, in the back hall."

I thanked her and retraced my earlier steps. Next to the fire extinguisher, a small corkboard held a list of task assignments for the week and a lined sheet of paper hand ruled into three columns. The first was for dates. The second held start and end times. The third gave the name of the person who would be using the car.

I ran my finger up to the date of Delozier's murder. Nurse Wellington had signed up to use the car from five to ten p.m. But what if she'd stayed out later? Or what if someone else had used it after her?

***

I had other clients to see to, so it wasn't until I'd made a few phone calls and typed up some invoices that I settled down and thought about that morning's developments.

I didn't buy Freeze's idea of blackmail. From what I'd learned about Delozier, he was too lazy to concoct something that elaborate let alone carry it through. He was a fast buck kind of guy. On the other hand, I had no doubt he was the one who stuck the matchbook in the ivy. His laziness had come into play there too, as did stealth. He'd stood there in that hidden spot a few steps from the side door and talked to someone who lived there, or possibly worked there. The question was, who?

At the moment I was no closer to an answer than I had been when I first met the Barretts, so I went across the street and had a cup of coffee at a nondescript little place that served the best brew in town. Fortified, I headed back into the field of battle.

As I pulled into the parking area at the side of the house, Simon Barrett and his nail chewing assistant, McDowell, were getting out of their car.

"Ah, Miss Sullivan. Haven't we driven you off yet?"

Beneath his sea captain's beard, Simon's smile was all charm and amiability. I reminded myself that a man didn't get to be a business tycoon of his caliber by being a pussycat.

"No, you'll have to try harder."

He laughed and swept the door to the back hall open. "I need to see what Jack's been up to, so John and I will sneak in this way too."

The light mood faded when we got inside. Jack's door stood wide open, and Jack and Noah were engaged in a terse conversation. By the looks of it the two brothers were one raised voice away from blows.

"No, I don't know if the call from Washington has come through," Noah snapped, catching sight of his father. "I've been away from my desk for five minutes, so it probably has." He stalked back toward their office wing.

Simon raised an eyebrow at his younger son who shrugged in irritation. His voice, however, was modulated.

"The reports from France are better than expected. The jumble after the liberation of Paris has settled considerably. Farmers have been able to assess damages. Cuba's production continues strong as ever. Your copies are right here."

Pivoting, he retrieved a sheaf of papers from his desk and handed them to his father just as Kaye came tripping down the stairs.

"Oh, hello," she said to me with her usual cheer. "Jack, have you any letters—?"

"Yes. I'll be right in."

The poor woman's long face drooped at his abruptness. Simon and his assistant had paused across the way at the loveseats outside the living room. Arlene and Tinker were tucked up there. Simon's voice was an indistinct murmur as he spoke to his daughter.

"What did you need?" Jack's question to me strained to be civil.

Residue from whatever differences he and Noah had been having hung in the air. I shook my head. It wasn't the most productive time for asking him something.

"It can wait."

He gave a distracted nod and turned back to his office, where Kaye had a steno pad out awaiting dictation.

It had occurred to me it might be fun to ask Tinker and Arlene about the Little Red Tavern and watch their reactions.

"What now?" asked Tinker as I joined them.

Before I could answer, Simon Barrett raced back into view.

"Get Nurse Wellington!" he shouted. "Judith has been strangled. She's not moving."

CHAPTER TWENTY-SIX

Arlene was the first to recover from the momentary paralysis. Jackknifing off the loveseat she raced for the stairs. I ran toward the offices where Judith had been found, following Simon. On the way, I realized I had never been in this part of the house and might be as unwelcome in what apparently was a restricted area as the police had been. If so, the man in front of me could tell me to stay out. Those were the very words he snapped at those behind us even as he motioned me through a door into one of the offices.

"Over here."

The room we were in provided generous space for two desks. The first, with a connecting table holding a typewriter, clearly belonged to Judith. Further back, Noah leaned against a second desk. His hand rubbed back and forth across his mouth. At the rear, the door to a connecting office stood open.

Judith lay sprawled face down between two desks. Her black hair had come unpinned on one side and spilled over her shoulder. There was a rope around her neck. She lay very still.

"She has a pulse," McDowell said, looking up from where he knelt beside her.

His levelheadedness surprised me given how nervous he'd been on other occasions. As I bent for a closer look, I caught a whiff of something sweet. It was chloroform.

With a ripping cough, Judith rolled over. She gasped and clawed at her neck. Red welts showed where the rope encircling it had rubbed or bitten in.

"Wait," I said as McDowell reached for the ends of it. The rope wouldn't yield any fingerprints but the way it was tied might tell the police something.

"Everyone move away from her." Nurse Wellington bristled with indignation as she bustled in. "You too," she said to me.

Judith lurched to a sitting position. "Oh! Spinning. Dizzy…" She fumbled at the rope. "I can't…" She coughed. "I can't breathe!"

"It's panic. You're perfectly fine," Nurse Wellington said as she took her pulse. "Just try and relax."

The rope had been crossed at the back of her neck and twisted a couple of times. It was already slipping. I reached past Nurse Wellington and removed it, earning a glare.

"Noah, I need a manila envelope, the largest you have," I said.

He didn't respond. He seemed frozen in place. "I found her. She was lying there and I nearly tripped. I thought she was…"

"Noah! The envelope," his father said sharply.

It stirred him to action.

"Judith, what happened?" Simon, kneeling beside her, took her hand and chafed it.

"He came up behind me… I noticed the window was open and went to close it and… I never saw him. He grabbed me and held his hand over my mouth and nose, and I got woozy. And then I think he must've shoved me, and then he had something around my neck and was choking me!" She looked around as if noticing us for the first time. "The lab. Did he get in there?"

"I'd just gone in when I heard Mr. Barrett," McDowell said. "It was locked when I got there. I'll check whether anything's been disturbed." He hurried off.

"Let's get you in to a couch," said Simon.

"She needs to stay where she is a bit longer—" began Nurse Wellington.

"No, I'm fine, really. Just awfully, awfully dizzy."

Nurse Wellington's lips pressed together. She was giving her patient very close scrutiny.

"I'm not sure I can walk on my own though," Judith was saying.

I dropped the rope into the envelope. Simon and Noah helped Judith to her feet. She swayed and put a hand to her head then, leaning heavily against Simon, she gave a plucky smile as the two men half led, half carried her from the room. Nurse Wellington, having studied her with a practiced eye, went ahead of them.

Since no one seemed to have noticed I wasn't tagging along, I took the opportunity to make a quick scan of my surroundings. I didn't see anything that might point to the intruder's identity. No matchbook covers, business cards, or pack of cigarettes dropped in the shuffle. Judith had mentioned coming in and finding the window open. I wondered where she'd been. Presumably, the window currently half open was the one she had noticed. I went to it and looked out. An easy jump in for anyone in reasonable physical shape. Using my hanky, I closed the window and locked it. Then I snatched tape and a sheet of blank paper from Judith's desk and secured the paper over the latch. Hopefully, it would convey the message not to touch it.

By the time I reached the living room they were settling Judith onto one of the loveseats. Those who had been excluded from Simon's offices – Tinker and Jack and Kaye Archer – crowded around exclaiming and asking questions. Griggs had reappeared and stood in the background.

"Move back. She needs room to breathe," ordered the nurse.

"Please, could I have some water?"

"That wouldn't be a good idea," warned Nurse Wellington.

Judith blinked and looked from the nurse in her uniform to the rest of us and back again as if taking things in for the first time. She put out a trembling hand. "Go back to Helen!" she said in a shrill voice. "I'm perfectly fine, but Helen's not safe. Don't you see? None of us are safe!"

"Would you like some coffee?" I suggested. "You're not making much sense at the moment."

Simon was frowning. His secretary grew contrite.

"Yes. Coffee. To clear the cobwebs." Griggs hurried to get some. "But I'm so thirsty."

"She's not going to choke. There's no reason why she shouldn't have a drink of water," said Simon.

He snatched a glass from a nearby tray and half-filled the tumbler. Nurse Wellington opened her mouth to argue again but then subsided. Judith drank thirstily.

"I'm sorry I've made such a scene, Simon, but can't you see?" Her composure was returning. She set the glass aside. "It's what I thought when we found out that man Delozier had been killed. Someone has it in for this family. First poor Charlotte, then him, and just now…" She raised a hand to the red marks on her neck.

"Delozier wasn't part of the family. He was hired help," Noah snapped. Unspoken was the implication that Judith held the same status. "What she's suggesting is ridiculous."

Judith's cheeks flamed. "It's not! Are you going to wait until someone else in the house is killed? What if whoever attacked me is still in the house?"

Simons eyes slid toward the upstairs and his nearly helpless wife.

"I can go up and stay with Helen and tell her what's happening if you'd like to have Nurse Wellington on hand down here a bit longer," I offered.

Since I already had questions I wanted to ask the nurse, getting her reaction to Judith's behavior and whatever happened after I left might be interesting. Besides, it had been some days since I checked in with Helen.

***

Arlene was curled on her mother's bed, leaning against her and holding her hand when I entered.

"Everything's fine downstairs," I said with a smile. "Judith had a bit of a scare, but she was sitting in the living room having coffee when I came up."

"Arlene said she was attacked."

"An intruder may have frightened her, but she wasn't injured in the least."

They peppered me with questions. Before I could get a word in to answer any of them, Lola Price burst in.

"What's this about Judith being attacked?"

She must have run up the stairs. She was out of breath. When she had pulled up a chair close to Helen, I gave them the highlights. My account was generously edited.

I had just gotten to Judith's interest in coffee to help clear her brain when Nurse Wellington whisked in.

"Pulse, Helen."

Her patient presented her wrist with ease born of practice. She opened her mouth to ask me a question. The nurse shushed her.

"Well, did I pass?" Helen asked when the nurse stepped back.

"Steady as a rock."

Helen smiled. "Then why don't you take a break? You've been lending a hand with the situation downstairs. I have three people here to pamper me and raise the alarm if I need anything. Put your feet up. Enjoy a cup of tea. Read the paper. You deserve a change of scene."

Nurse Wellington hesitated. "Miss Todd seems to think her attacker might still be in the house and might have a go at someone else."

"Poppycock. If someone was surprised in the midst of whatever crime they meant to commit, which appears to be the case downstairs, they're hardly going to sneak all the way up here to attempt something else. Go on. Enjoy yourself."

I got to my feet. "I have things to do at the office, but I think you're well protected."

With a grin, Arlene shifted to a cross-legged position. "Hearts, ladies?"

Lola cocked an eyebrow at her. "You realize you always lose."

"Prepare to be skunked."

CHAPTER TWENTY-SEVEN

I caught up with Nurse Wellington in the hallway.

"I have a question."

"Don't we all," she muttered under her breath. "About the uproar downstairs, I presume?"

"Yes. I'm curious why you tried to stop them when Judith asked for water."

The woman in her starched uniform drew up as sharply as if she'd slammed into a wall. "Because people with chloroform are prone to vomiting when they wake up, even on an empty stomach."

I nodded. "That was my experience when it happened to me."

Her manner, which had grown defensive, relaxed. We walked toward the back stairs together.

"I take it she kept the coffee down okay?"

"She did."

"Could she have received such a small dose it didn't affect her?"

"Possibly."

The clipped answer suggested she had other ideas. Although I stayed silent, my presence at her side told her I didn't intend to let the subject drop. I waited for her to continue.

"Or she might have staged her little drama to get attention."

"From whom?"

"Mr. Barrett. I've been part of the household long enough to see how eager she is for him to notice her as something other than a secretary. She notes his preferences in food and activities, the things that annoy him." She paused. "I believe she anticipates Helen's death and is eager to take on the role of wife."

I digested it. Arlene harbored thoughts along the same lines, but I had dismissed them as anger at the thought of anyone taking her mother's place.

"Is that likely?" I asked. "Helen's death?"

We were at the back stairs. Peering down to make sure no one overheard us, she lowered her voice.

"I don't know. Some days she seems to be making progress. Other days she's… exhausted. Weak." Her voice was sad. "When I first came here a little over a year ago and started her on new therapies, I could see her growing stronger by the day. Then all at once she went downhill. I discovered recently that there'd been a pharmacy error in a prescription, and I hoped…"

Emotion overcame her. Retracing a few steps, she sank onto one of the benches placed along the hallway and dabbed at her eyes with a hanky. Her professional shell had cracked.

"Nurse Wellington?"

"If it hadn't been for that sweet young woman, I might never have checked at the pharmacy."

I stood stock still. "What young woman?"

"Miss Littlefield. In the upset over her death... the police... trying to keep Helen on an even keel... I completely forgot. And she'll never know that she helped."

"Nurse Wellington, what did Charlotte do? Or say?"

"It was so whimsical." She cleared her throat, regaining control of herself. "I dismissed it at the time. She was young, and very fond of Helen, and saw how the least exertion was wearing on her. I knew she meant well. She said maybe I should take all Helen's pill bottles to the druggist and make sure they contained what they were supposed to. She said she'd read a story once in a magazine about a woman almost dying because they'd mixed her prescription up with someone else's."

"When was this?"

"I think perhaps the day before she died. No more than two."

"And at some point you checked and there had been an error?"

"Yes. The bottle for one of her heart medications held pills for hay fever instead. Their appearance is identical."

CHAPTER TWENTY-EIGHT

Charlotte Littlefield had seen something – or maybe someone – as nearly as Mrs. Salmon could make out from the girl's last, frantic phone call. My talk with Nurse Wellington left me suspecting it might have been both.

Let's say Charlotte had seen someone tampering with Helen's pill bottle. Maybe she'd recognized who it was, maybe she hadn't. Whichever the case, the culprit had become aware of her presence. Presto. One motive for murder.

Time to work backwards again. Killing Charlotte was a foolproof way to hide the fact they were attempting to kill Helen. What other reason would they have for seeing she got the wrong medication? Based on what both the nurse and Arlene thought, Judith seemed the likeliest candidate. But Judith might simply be an opportunist.

Chatting about other things, I walked downstairs with Nurse Wellington. We parted ways when she went into the kitchen for the cup of tea Helen had suggested. I drifted down to the list showing who had taken the shared car out and when. Two days before Charlotte was killed, Helen and Nurse Wellington had been away at a doctor's appointment for several hours. A fine time for someone to go into Helen's room and make a quick substitution in one of her pill bottles.

I ran my finger down to the night Delozier was murdered, to where Nurse Wellington had signed the car out and signed it back in. With all that had gone on today, I wanted to type my notes up while things were fresh in my mind. Talking to Hays to confirm what the nurse had told me could wait until tomorrow.

***

"That's right. If any of them use that shared car and get back after, oh, nine-thirty at night, they park it at the bottom of the drive so they don't wake Mrs. Barrett. I guess she wakes really easy and has trouble falling off again. They lock it and leave it down there and I bring it up first thing in the morning before anyone needs it."

Hays was already into the nondriving part of his chauffeuring duties when I arrived on Tuesday. He seemed glad to take a break from buffing a wax job on the other car, the one used for business. He leaned against a corner of the main garage, face lifted to the morning sun, although it caused him to squint.

"What about this car? Does it ever go out in the evening?"

"Nope. Mr. Barrett's real strict about it. He says since the government allowed them to have a separate car for the business – because of whatever he and Mr. McDowell are doing here – he's not going to take advantage of it even a little. He's like that. Conscientious. And he keeps records on it. Where it goes each trip, how many miles and that."

"What if he needs to go to a meeting at night?"

Hays shook his head. "He doesn't. Mrs. Randall says he and Mrs. Barrett make it a point to have dinner together. Most nights he and Mr. McDowell go back after to work in their offices. But the car gets put up at six o'clock, always."

"Put up where?"

"Right here in the garage." He gave a grin. "I have a nice little apartment right above it. I may not be as light a sleeper as Mrs. Barrett is, but if that car went out, I would know it, if that's what you're thinking."

That settled that. I hoped I'd have better luck inside.

***

"I'm sorry to interrupt," I said when Kaye came down to join me in the small sitting room where I'd first questioned family members. It seemed like months ago rather than only twelve days.

"Oh, don't apologize. Helen's been dictating like a mad woman. We both were ready for a break."

"She must be feeling well today."

"Downright feisty. It's wonderful to see her like this. If only… Well, that's beside the point. You have questions?"

"I am a basket of questions."

As was often the case when she was amused, she covered her mouth and tittered.

"Do you mind if we go outside?" On the terrace I would have my choice of spots where I could stand and see anyone approaching before we could be overheard.

It was too early for lunch preparations and neither Tinker nor Arlene was in evidence. The flowers in the planters glistened from watering.

"Oh, this is lovely. I face a mountain of typing when I go back in," Kaye said with a note of bliss in her voice.

"It's about the night that Jimmy Delozier was murdered. It was also Nurse Wellington's night off."

"Oh yes. Well, not her usual night. Usually she likes Sunday off, but her friend's a nurse too and she was taking someone else's shift on Sunday and they wanted to go to a movie, so they went then. Dinner too. That's what they do. Now, your questions?"

Sometimes Kaye's fondness for details set my teeth on edge.

"Do you recall what time Nurse Wellington got home?"

"Nine thirty-ish. Somewhere between nine thirty and ten, but certainly no later than ten. She's always back by then. Helen was sleeping away so we whispered goodnight and went to our rooms."

"I understand about parking down by the street so as not to wake Mrs. Barrett, but what about people sleeping in bedrooms on the other side of the house near the driveway? Could a car pulling in and parking down there waken them?"

"Oh, I expect so. My room is up on the third floor and I occasionally…" She frowned. "Ummm…"

"What?"

"The night we've been talking about, it was stuffy so I had my windows open. It was one of those toss and turn nights, and somewhere in the middle of it I thought – no, I'm reasonably certain – that I heard a car pull in at the foot of the drive and turn off the engine. I suppose it must've been Arlene coming in. A few minutes later I did hear footsteps and the side door being eased closed, and she sneaks in that way when she's out especially late. She's an awfully good kid at heart, really, but she is a bit wild. Except… when Pammy drives her home, Pammy doesn't usually turn off the engine."

"Possibly it was one of the servants coming in early," I said to deflect her interest while my own kicked into high gear. "Or maybe Mr. Barrett's assistant wanting to get an early start on something."

"Yes, possibly." Her frown eased. "Mr. McDowell does seem to push himself. According to Helen, Mr. Barrett's very worried about how little sleep he gets, poor man. You can see from his nails that his nerves are a mess."

"Who else sleeps on that side of the house?"

"Arlene, but she was out. Nurse Wellington is in the next room so she's within easy reach of Helen. The next room is the one Charlotte was in, and the big one at the front is Tinker and Noah."

I thanked her and went in search of Tinker. Griggs thought she was up in her room and sent one of the maids to tell her I wanted to see her. Given her antipathy toward me I decided not to hold my breath. To my surprise she came down, and rather promptly at that.

"Make it quick," she said. "I have to get ready for a charity luncheon. I'm on the board. A pale substitute for Helen, of course." She made no effort to hide her bitterness.

"Did anyone tell you that?"

"No, of course not."

"You overheard whispers?"

She reddened. "What's your point?"

I shrugged. "Only that they might think you're perfectly ducky. Shall we go into that little sitting room?"

With a glare she led the way.

"Since you have things to do, I'll get right to the point. When you're in your bedroom can you hear cars coming in and out of the drive?"

"Of course. We're right next to it."

"What about a car parking down at the foot of the drive? Or one starting up down there. Can you hear that?"

Her manner grew wary. "What are you trying to pin on us now?"

"The night that Nurse Wellington had her night off, someone took the car out after she returned."

"Well, it wasn't me!"

"I wasn't implying that. I just want to know if you heard it and could possibly tell me roughly what time it was."

Tinker ran a hand through her short hair leaving it on end. She began to pick at her bangle, which today was an exquisite circle of gold and ivory. When she fiddled with her bracelet, it meant she was nervous, I realized, like she'd been the very first time I talked to her, here in this room.

"I didn't hear anything! I didn't!" She looked at me fiercely, but her eyes had a glaze of misery and unshed tears.

Nervous, I wondered now, or scared?

"Tinker," I said softly. "What is it you're not telling me?"

"I…" She hiccupped back her distress. "I didn't hear anything, honestly, but… Noah didn't come to bed that night," she finished in a rush.

I recognized a woman who needed to share a burden. Though I hadn't seen it before, Tinker was as isolated in her own way as Arlene was. They spent time together because neither was overrun with friends of their own age. No doubt they shared confidences, but this got into territories she wouldn't want to share with her much younger sister-in-law.

"They seem to work very long hours some nights, Noah and his father. Isn't it possible he fell asleep on a couch, or maybe stretched out there because he didn't want to disturb you?"

I felt like a louse, offering reassurance even as my mind raced ahead with the implications of what she had told me. Tinker's gaze was fixed on her bracelet. She traced a finger along the inside surface, causing the pretty bangle to revolve.

"I guess. Yes. Only…" She swallowed. "He's… It's like I don't even know him since right before Charlotte's accident. He and Jack had a big blowup and he, he hasn't been the same since."

"He and Jack had a fight?" Here was something new.

"A quarrel."

"Okay, quarrel. Do you know what it was over?"

She nodded. When she raised her eyes the moisture in them had started to spill. "Over me."

CHAPTER TWENTY-NINE

It was still only midmorning. I needed time to digest what I'd learned about the quarrel between the Barrett brothers. If nothing else, it raised the possibility that Noah had been out the night of the Delozier murder. Even worse was the possibility the quarrel was tied to one or both of the deaths that had afflicted their household. Although Judith's hysteria yesterday had been overblown, she did appear to be right about one thing: Two people with ties to the Barretts had been marked for murder.

While I gave my brain cells a chance to grapple with this latest development, I set course for the Little Red Tavern. It was early enough that they wouldn't be busy with a lunchtime drinking crowd yet, and late enough for me to have a drink to compensate for taking up some of their time. Given the tawdry nature of a few undertakings by Arlene and Pammy, they were the likeliest candidates for venturing into the place. I still had their photographs from when I checked on their story about volunteering at the USO, so I took them along. In view of how Arlene seemed to have changed in the last few days, I found myself hoping the photographs would prove useless.

Today there were no police cars in evidence. In fact, there were only two other cars waiting for my DeSoto to join them. When I'd made my way past the painted can-can girls still kicking away on the front of the building, I found myself in a cozy, clean-as-a-whistle pub. Three old codgers trading sections of newspaper at a table with beer bottles at their elbows didn't even look up when I came in.

Given the diminutive size of the place, I felt certain the man wiping glasses behind the bar was the owner. He had a pair of cowlicks framing the bald upper part of his head. They gave him an owl-like look.

"What'll it be?" he asked as I slid onto a stool near where he was working.

"How about a Guinness?"

"Sure." Giving me the once over, he put a glass under the tap. "What are you selling?"

"I'm hoping to be on the other end. I'm after some information on Jimmy Delozier."

He scowled, less amiable now. "We already talked to the cops."

"I'm not the police. I'm looking into another matter the police aren't showing any interest in."

Not strictly true, but close enough for my flexible conscience. I slid one of my business cards across the bar to him. A woman who'd been ladling pickled eggs into a gallon jar at the opposite end came to look at it with him. Her upper arms were sturdy as tree trunks. Taking the picture of Arlene and Pammy from its envelope, I turned it toward them.

"Ever see Delozier with either of these two?"

"Nope," said the owner. "I never saw him with a woman, period."

"Not unless you count the one old enough to be his mother." His wife grinned.

"What? When was that?" asked the man.

"I don't rightly remember. A week or so before that hit-skip the police asked about. We were busy that night and they were back in the corner. I might not have seen 'em myself if I hadn't been serving."

"You never said anything to me. Did you tell the cops?"

"It slipped my mind with you, and no, I didn't tell the cops. That one in charge rubbed me the wrong way, telling me not to get rattled, to do my best, like I was twelve years old. Besides, they wouldn't have been interested. They wanted to know about girlfriends, did I know if he had one, had I seen him in here with a girl he seemed interested in. The woman I saw was too old to interest someone like Jimmy. She dressed nice, looked like she didn't like to be here. I did wonder if she might be his mother or aunt or something like that."

"Why?" I asked before her husband could start

quizzing her again, or maybe giving advice she didn't want.

The owner's wife planted her sizable elbows on the bar, pleased with her audience of two.

"She gave him some money," she said, directly to me. "Slid it to him in an envelope. He counted it."

"That's the sort he was," put in her husband. "Never gave two hoots about being polite."

"He counted it," resumed his wife. "Then they talked some more."

***

Who was old enough to fit the description of the woman Delozier had been with at the Little Red Tavern? Leaning back in my office chair, I doodled at one edge of the lines on my tablet then started a list.

Helen couldn't walk, let alone drive a car.

Lola? Definitely. *I would crawl over broken glass for Helen.*

Judith? Possibly. Or was she too young?

Nurse Wellington? She earned a good salary and might dress smartly when she wasn't in her nurse's uniform.

In the course of my work, I'd brushed elbows with other wealthy clients. At holidays, and sometimes other special occasions, they brought a photographer in to capture the entire group. Sometimes a few valued members of staff were included as well. Secretaries, a nurse, an elderly relative's paid companion, for example.

After a moment's more thought, I called the intrepid Kaye. "I need a photograph, or photographs, of the Barretts, preferably with as many other members of the household as you can find. Can you get me something like that?"

"Well, yes. At least I think so. Would Mrs. Price—?"

"Yes, include Lola, definitely. You, Judith, the nurse. It's the women I'm interested in, primarily."

"What are you going to do with them? The photographs?"

Her curiosity was tinged with eagerness to be in the know about something exciting. I kept my answer light.

"If I told you that, I wouldn't be living up to the 'private' part of private investigator, would I?"

Instead of her awkward titter I got a small sigh. "All right. I'll rustle them up."

"And keep it between the two of us, will you?"

"Oh. Okay."

As I hung up, I again considered the list in front of me. Reluctantly, I added one more possibility:

Mrs. Salmon.

My phone rang.

"This is Jack," said the caller. "Um, Jack Barrett. I know it's spur of the moment, but I was wondering if

I might take you to lunch. You wanted to talk to me yesterday, but Noah and I were having words. And then there was that business with Judith."

I told him I'd be delighted. He picked me up in a taxi.

"I hope you don't mind not going to the club," he said as I got in.

I assumed he meant the country club.

"The food's quite good here and there's not likely to be anyone I know coming up to interrupt or offer condolences," he said when I'd assured him I didn't mind in the least. He smiled faintly. "Charlotte liked it."

It was on a side street, an Italian place. The owner patted Jack on the shoulder as he greeted him. "You doing okay, Mr. Barrett? We've missed you."

The waiter arrived before we'd been seated. He too made a fuss over Jack. When we had ordered and been supplied from a straw-wrapped bottle of red wine, Jack leaned back in his chair.

"What did you do to set Pammy Witherspoon on the warpath?"

"Breathed, probably. Why?"

"As I was leaving, she came tearing in and demanded to know if you were there. She said you are nothing but a cheap troublemaker and we'd be sorry we hired you. I told her she was wrong about the cheap part. She didn't seem to find it amusing."

I grinned broadly. "Did she indicate the nature of her grievance?"

"She said you'd ruined her life and that you'd be sorry. Or maybe we were the ones she said would be sorry. Then she started shouting for Arlene, calling her a whiny little baby. I tried to tell her Arlene wasn't home, but I don't think she even heard. She started upstairs yelling that Arlene couldn't hide. Poor Griggs didn't know what to do."

"And was Arlene trying to avoid her?"

"Nope. She's down at the university, and having a fine time by the sounds of it. She'd called earlier to say she wouldn't be home for lunch and to ask if we still had her old archery equipment from the last summer she went to camp."

I made a show of raising my eyebrows. "She's going to fend off attacks from Pammy with a bow and arrows?"

He chuckled as plates of steaming pasta slid in front of each of us. "Nothing quite so drastic, I'm sure. Mother told me about it when I went up to say goodbye to her. She said it was rather muddled. Something about a girl Arlene had met in class and activities for children whose mothers work in defense plants. Mother said she hadn't heard Arlene sound so excited since she came home."

"While I don't recommend an arrow through Pammy as a solution, Arlene would be wise to avoid her for a few days if she possibly can." Forever would be better, I thought. "Pammy is... unpredictable. I've seen her in action. I suspect the police may have paid her a visit that set her off."

His chewing came to a standstill. "Not about Charlotte surely."

"It might have to do with gambling debts she's run up and the men who want them paid." I smiled. "I hear things."

It had the desired effect of pointing him in a different direction. "Is my sister mixed up...?"

"Only in that she pointed me to the burlesque theater where Pammy's working so she can pay off her debt."

Jack looked dazed. "Wow. But I don't suppose it was Pammy you wanted to ask me about." He cocked his head. "Is it?"

"No." Reluctantly I took a break from my veal scaloppini. "I want to know what you can tell me about the Little Red Tavern."

His expression registered nothing but mild curiosity. "Nothing, I'm afraid. Is it an actual tavern, or a book or what?"

"A place. I was hoping you and Charlotte might have gone there, or that you'd heard her mention it."

"No, sorry. Why?"

"The name came up. In connection with Jimmy Delozier. I figured it was a long shot. But there's something else."

"Okay." He touched his coffee cup to ask if I was ready and signaled our waiter.

"The disagreement you and Noah were having yesterday when your father and Mr. McDowell and I came in, was that a continuation of the quarrel you had over Tinker not long before Charlotte was killed?"

He sat back so abruptly the cane hooked to the back of his chair clattered to the floor.

CHAPTER THIRTY

The waiter scurried to retrieve the cane. When we were alone again, Jack stared at me.

"How did— What do you know—?"

"Tinker told me. She said the two of you quarreled over her, but she wouldn't say why."

Expelling an angry breath, he turned his head to the side. "Because my brother is an idiot."

"Maybe you could be more specific?"

"All right, all right. I'm not sure what day it was, but as you said, not long before Charlotte was killed. I had a pair of shoes resoled. I don't know what the cobbler had done to them, but my knees were aching, my hips were aching. I went upstairs to put on a different pair. When I came back out, I heard someone crying, little tiny sobs like you try to hide. It was coming from Noah and Tinker's room. Probably I should have kept my nose out, but she sounded so miserable.

"I tapped on the door. She said to go away, but that doesn't always mean someone wants you to. Arlene's like that. I peeked in and she was sitting there on the bed with her shoulders all hunched up and her arms around her knees."

"Tinker, you mean."

"Yes. She's little anyway, and she looked like a child. Lost. Forlorn. She looked so miserable. I went over and sat beside her and put my arm around her and said hey, what's wrong? And she said nothing, she was just feeling sorry for herself."

Our coffee arrived, accompanied by a plate of little cookies. When we were alone again, Jack looked at me earnestly.

"It seemed like the most natural thing in the world, comforting her. It still does."

I nodded. I had a hunch I knew where this was headed before he confirmed it, I wanted to get some more information.

"Did she say why?"

"In a jumbled sort of way." Jack stirred sugar into his coffee. "It was pretty clear she felt neglected. She said Noah never had time for her anymore. I told her we were all working long hours, that the powers that be thought the war was coming close to the end and that the Axis powers would turn even nastier as they got desperate. I told her I thought Dad and Noah were working on something that would protect American troops."

He shot me a guilty look.

"I probably shouldn't have said that, to either of

you, but I'm so damn tired of it all. Anyway, Tinker said no, that Noah had just lost interest in her. She said… She said they hadn't been intimate in weeks. Then she asked me to be honest and tell her if there was another woman."

"And is there? Was there?"

"Of course not. I tried to kid her out of the notion. I asked her when on earth she thought he'd have time for that, and said 'Tinker you're an attractive woman'. Unfortunately, that was exactly when the door opened—"

"—and Noah walked in."

His unhappy nod confirmed it.

"Things got quite ugly, as you can imagine. He grabbed me by the collar and jerked me up and shouted at me that he'd punch my face except the whole family would turn on him for breaking my poor little bones. He told me if I wanted to cheat on Charlotte before we were even married, that was my business, but not to try it with his wife.

"I tried to tell him it wasn't what he thought. So did Tinker. Sure, I had my arm around her, but we were just talking. We both had all our clothes on, for heaven's sake. I've made attempts since then, most recently yesterday. He won't listen. The worst part is I've probably made things worse for Tinker."

With a quick apology he then excused himself to use the phone. Kaye had agreed to mind his office while he was out and he wanted to let her know he was running late but was on the way back. The check had arrived by the time he returned. We didn't resume our conversation until we were out of the restaurant.

"You wouldn't be asking this if you didn't think our set-to might've had something to do with Charlotte, or what happened to her. You're not suggesting the two of them got involved, are you? They didn't. They wouldn't."

"I wasn't considering that at all. I did wonder if what happened with Tinker might have made your brother angry enough to try and settle scores somehow."

A stricken look entered his eyes as my meaning sank in. "You mean angry enough to run Charlotte down?"

"Or to hire someone. Possibly Delozier."

He stood like a statue there on the sidewalk as people moved past and around us. At length he shook his head. He put his hand out to beckon an approaching taxi.

"My brother thinks of everything in terms of himself. Is he being slighted, is he getting his fair share. It would never cross his mind that his wife was lonely, and starved for just a little simple affection. He's self-centered and loses his temper and sulks like a child when things don't go his way. But he's not a murderer."

***

At my request, Jack had asked whether Arlene was home yet when he called Kaye from the restaurant. She reported that his sister wasn't expected until mid-afternoon. When the taxi, which was his main form of transportation since he couldn't drive, dropped me off at my office, I went upstairs and powdered my nose. Then I walked to my own car and set course for the University of Dayton with more than moderate expectation that Arlene would be where she said she was these days.

The university for most of its life had been known as St. Mary's College. It was south of downtown, east of Main on Stewart Street. Trying to locate Arlene on a good-sized campus with numerous buildings when she wasn't expecting me might be just a step or two removed from hunting a needle in a haystack. There were worse things to do on a nice spring day than take my time strolling green lawns and enjoying the sunshine.

Two places seemed like the likeliest spot to find Arlene, the student lounge or the library. It was a coin toss which she might favor. The library called heads and won so I tried there first. It was a handsome building of red brick with a few miles of lawn in front of it and six white columns guarding the entry. After passing the scrutiny of the woman at the front desk, I wandered around looking for Arlene's blond head. There were a lot of blonds. When I was on the verge of giving up, I spotted her at a table in the corner. Several fat books were stacked at her elbow and she was scribbling away on the topmost of several sheets of paper. The other five chairs at the table were unoccupied. I stood for several moments before she noticed me and looked up.

"Oh. Hi." She squinted her eyes and opened them twice like someone bothered by light. "Is anything wrong? What are you doing here?"

"Nothing's wrong. I have some questions and thought you might be more comfortable talking here than at your house." I waggled my hand as she turned wary. "It's nothing awful and it's not about you, it's about something you might have heard. Can we go outside?"

For several seconds, her wariness persisted. Then she gave a curt nod. "I guess. It's time for me to leave anyway."

She gathered her things and we walked out together through rows of wooden tables where other students bent their heads over books. There wasn't a low wall or bench to sit on outside the library, so we walked.

"I take it you like it down here," I said. "What, all of two days, and Jack says you're going to be coaching an archery team?"

"Nothing quite as grand as that. A girl in the

chemistry class I'm auditing – because it's too late in the term to take it for credit – had wrist guards with her this morning. They're leather. You lace them up on your wrists so the bow string doesn't burn you when you release it." She gestured. "I asked if there was a PE class in archery. She laughed and said no, she helped three days a week with a program for kids whose mothers work in defense plants. Her part's archery. And don't think I can't see you're trying to soften me up. What is it you wanted to ask? I have a trolley to catch."

As she spoke she was consulting her wristwatch. It was the first time I'd seen her wear one. The brown leather strap was such a contrast to Tinker's pretty bracelets that I smiled.

"I could give you a ride."

"While you give me the third degree?" she asked, but her mouth twitched.

"Maybe just the second. My car's there."

We both rolled our windows down when we got in. Arlene rested her elbow in the window well and turned slightly so she could watch me.

"You said inside you wanted to know about something I'd heard."

"That you possibly heard," I corrected. "Your bedroom's on the side of the house that's by the driveway, right?"

"You know it is. You've been in my room."

"Do you hear cars coming in and out?"

"Of course. I'm at the back where the garages are."

"What about when someone comes in late enough that they park at the bottom of the drive? Do you hear them turn the engine off?"

She pushed her bottom lip out in thought. "I don't believe so, no. I mean I've never heard a noise and thought 'Oh, that's someone pulling into the parking space down by the street.'"

Discouraging, but I wasn't ready to give up just yet. "What about a car starting up down there? Have you ever heard that?"

"Well, that would be the same, wouldn't it? If I couldn't hear one, I wouldn't hear the other."

"So you've never heard Pammy leave, for example, when she'd brought you home."

Arlene snorted. "From my room? Are you kidding? Pammy takes off before I've gone two steps. It's a miracle she's never knocked me down. Why all this interest? What's this about?"

"I have reason to think someone might have driven the car that parks down there late the night Jimmy Delozier was killed." That reason was nothing beyond my own theory, but Arlene didn't know that.

"You think one of us killed him?"

"No. I think somebody in the house went to meet him and found him dead, or saw him get killed."

The girl beside me was silent. Her lower lip moved in and out. "Pull over."

CHAPTER THIRTY-ONE

"Arlene, what's wrong?" I didn't think I had offended her. Her request startled me.

"Just pull over. Please. It has nothing to do with what you're asking about, and I don't know if it's important, but something happened that was... well, it was odd. I think maybe you ought to know about it."

We were mere blocks from her home. Apparently, this was something she didn't want to discuss there, not even parked at the foot of the driveway. Whatever rapport I had established with her hung by the slenderest of threads. I turned into the first side street that looked promising and found a spot at the curb. Instead of speaking, I raised my eyebrows.

Arlene worked her lip in and out a couple more times, this time nibbling it like she had at Pammy's. She glanced at her watch again.

"I know you may not believe this." She sighed. "I've given you plenty of reason not to, not telling the truth about things. Plus you know I think Judith is a witch. I swear it's true, though. It's about last night."

"Last night?"

"I told you it wasn't about what you were interested in," she said defensively.

"Yes, okay. What about last night? Did you hear somebody come in? In a car?"

"No."

I struggled to keep my frustration at bay.

"When Jack took me down to the university for the first time, I ran into some people I knew, two girls I went to school with, and a fellow I'd met at parties with Pammy. He's not part of her crowd though. She thought he was dull. He isn't. He just doesn't drink himself silly and show off all the time. He can carry on an actual conversation. His left hand… Well, it's awful to look at, all red and pink and mangled. I think he fought in the war and they sent him back.

"Anyway, he took me to a play last night and afterwards we went for drinks. It was pretty late when I got home – after one I expect. I explained about cars waking Mother, so he let me out at our pull off and waited until I was halfway up before he went on."

An impish grin darted over her mouth. "I guess I got so used to sneaking in when I went out with Pammy that it's become a habit. I was creeping along in the grass at the side of the driveway when I saw the back door open and someone come out. It was Judith. She looked around as if she was about to do something and didn't want to be seen. I dropped down on my knees so she wouldn't see me."

She was getting to the crux of the story. I no longer begrudged the time it had taken. "I'm guessing she did do something?"

"Ohhh yes. She went to the trash can and spent about five minutes getting the lid off."

Easing it off so as not to make noise, I thought.

"Then she dropped something in. I couldn't see what, but it was white."

"I'll just bet you looked once she'd gone back in."

"Not right then in case she watched to make sure no one had seen. I stayed where I was for about twenty minutes. My foot went to sleep. Then, in case she heard me, I let myself in the front door, but quiet like I was trying to sneak in. Then I tiptoed to my room and changed into slacks and a black jersey and waited another twenty minutes."

Unlike the spot with the trellis where the matchbook had been discarded, the trash can might just be visible from inside the house. It was next to the side door used by the help, on the far side of the steps where it was mostly hidden. A person moving close to it would be easy to spot, however.

"I wanted to make sure she didn't see me if I poked my nose in," Arlene continued, "so I went across the hall and peeked through the keyhole in the door to her room." She squirmed. "I have done it before. Anyhow, I could make out that she was in bed, and it wasn't just a pillow stuffed under the sheets. I could hear her breathing. Not quite snoring, but right at the edge of it.

"Once I'd done that, I crept downstairs as fast as I could. I don't know what I expected to find in the trash or what I thought I could do with it. I guess I was thinking about the police because on the way out I detoured into the pantry and got one of the sterilized jars Cook keeps in there for making jelly."

This girl was smart and then some, I thought. I hoped she wasn't feeding me a line.

"I've read about fingerprints," she was saying. "The jar was the best I could think of, even though I wasn't sure it would hold whatever I found. I'd stuffed a pair of gloves in my pocket, too. When I got outside I took the lid off the trash can. It seemed like it took forever because I was trying not to make noise, but I didn't want to take so long I got caught either. I couldn't see very well, but I had a flashlight and I held that with my mouth and dug around as carefully as I could. There were scraps of white paper and wilted white flowers, but I finally found something else that was white and took it out. It was a handkerchief with something wrapped inside. I stuffed it into the jar, switched the flashlight off and took off."

"You didn't look to see what was in the handkerchief?"

"Not then. Not there. All I could think about was getting somewhere that no one would find me going through the trash. Well, I guess I was worried Judith might not have been sleeping after all. But when I did unwrap the handkerchief, you'll never guess what was inside."

***

Squeezing through the hedge at the far side of the Barretts' driveway left me with a tracery of fine red scratches on my forearms and legs. At least I'd had the foresight to take my stockings off and roll them up to leave in the car once Arlene told me where she'd stashed what she found in the trash and I agreed to meet her there.

"All quiet in the house," she reported as I dropped through a chest-high window at the back of the large garage used to store the cars that sat bereft of tires and awaiting the end of the war. "No sign of Judith, meaning she's working away in the lab office. Jack's in his office, and nobody upstairs will think twice if they saw me heading back here to sit in the garden."

Twenty minutes earlier as we drove the last few blocks to her house, Arlene had outlined what she thought was the best way of getting us both to the garage without being spotted. I had let her off at the end of the drive which she walked up as if coming from the bus stop. Leaving my car a block away, I had walked to the Barrett property and followed the hedge on the far side. At the back, where privet had grown for years through the wire fence abutting it, I'd pushed my way through greenery to reach the rear of the garage.

I had done a lot of walking. Now, in the unventilated enclosure, with sun beating down on its roof, my blouse clung damply to my skin. So did my hair. On a peg I saw what appeared to be a clean towel. Spreading it on an overturned bucket, I sat down.

"Okay. Where is this find of yours?"

Even to my own ears I sounded cranky. Arlene didn't seem to notice. She stood beside a blue and white Buick convertible with one hand resting on it affectionately.

"This is mine. My first car." She sighed.

If she simply opened the glove compartment, or even the trunk, I would be somewhat disappointed in the smart young woman I'd seen emerge in recent days. Instead, feeling her fingers along the finish, she went to the front and raised the hood.

"Here. See what you make of it." Joining me, she handed me a squat pint jar. Along with a pair of kid dress gloves. "I left them with it," she said noting my surprise. "It seemed like the efficient thing to do."

For both our sakes, I hoped the contents of the jar, which Arlene had told me about in the most general terms, proved worth looking at.

The gloves fit somewhat snugly, but allowed all the maneuverability I needed. When I had them on, I unscrewed the lid of the jar and removed a rolled up bundle of white cloth. It was, I saw as I undid it, a man's handkerchief.

A man's? Yet Judith had disposed of it.

Interesting.

Inside the handkerchief was a small bottle, about the size I bought Mercurochrome in to dab on scratches.

"I'm not sure what's in it. I didn't open it," Arlene said before I could ask. "They might have chemicals back there in the lab that wouldn't be smart to breathe. But that handkerchief reeks, and I recognized the smell."

So did I.

"Chloroform." The scent was faint now but unmistakable. Unfolding the fabric had stirred it up.

"She staged that whole business yesterday," Arlene said angrily. "Dabbed some on her chin or just on her clothes somewhere, and stashed that where it wouldn't be found."

"You don't know all that."

It made sense, though, and could be the reason Judith didn't get sick. The kind of simple oversight made by someone who knew the effect of a substance but not the reaction that followed. What baffled me was finding a motive. Could it really be what Nurse

Wellington had suggested? A bid for attention by a woman who thought her employer would soon be a widower? If that was true, then Judith's actions had nothing to do with Charlotte's murder or Delozier's. Except…

Old enough to be his mother… She gave him some money.

An entire horn section in my head replayed the words from my visit to the Little Red Tavern.

"May I take this? I want to give it to the police."

A second passed, followed by another. Arlene nodded.

As much as I looked forward to arm wrestling with Freeze, I was even keener to pay another visit to the Little Red Tavern.

CHAPTER THIRTY-TWO

"There ought to be a law against married detectives," Freeze grumbled. For other sections of the Dayton police, it was the end of the day shift, but most of the desks in the detective unit were occupied, some by men who had been there since morning and would be there well into the evening. The unfortunate man who had prompted Freeze's comment slunk past me, heading for the stairs and escape.

The ashtray next to the rumpled senior detective held such a mountain of butts and ashes that any addition seemed likely to cause an avalanche. Freeze eyed my entry with resignation. "What?"

"This." Taking the jar entrusted to me out of my handbag, I set it on his desk. "The jar was sterilized for making jelly or something, which probably doesn't matter two hoots, but Barrett's daughter thought it might. She wore gloves when she handled it and when she touched what's inside."

"Barrett's daughter? The spoiled little snip with the chip on her shoulder?"

"Yeah, Arlene can be a snot, but she's okay. She

was coming in late from a date last night and saw Barrett's secretary sneak out and look around to make sure nobody saw her and stuff that down in the trash."

Freeze stared at me for a moment. Then, removing a clean, pressed handkerchief of his own from a side drawer he unscrewed the top of the jar.

Boike had moseyed over. "You look like you've been through the mill – or is pouring water over your head some new beauty thing?"

I gave him a baleful look. "Ha."

Freeze had unwrapped the bottle. "So what am I supposed to be seeing here?"

"And smelling."

He lowered his nose to the spread out handkerchief, took a sniff, frowned, sniffed again. "Chloroform?"

I nodded.

"So? It's used in stuff that's manufactured, isn't it? Cleaning fluids and so on. Things like Barrett's company makes. And they've got some kind of auxiliary laboratory in back. Maybe somebody wiped up a spill. Is that what's in the bottle?"

"I don't know what's in it. Arlene, the daughter, didn't think it would be very smart to take a whiff in case it was something dangerous. Whatever it is, you don't slip out in the middle of the night to throw out something that spilled. Wait, hear me out, Freeze."

As quickly as I could, I summarized the incident of the previous afternoon in which in which Judith was found apparently chloroformed, with a rope around her neck. I told about her request for water and for coffee.

"So?" he said again. "Did they call the police about the attack, fake or otherwise? No? Then I don't see why you're bringing this to me."

Boike, on the other hand, was frowning over Judith's lack of nausea. He leaned his boxy shape back against his desk.

"I think she staged the whole thing to divert suspicion, or to lend support to a cockamamie idea she blathered about on how someone's got it in for the family – in which she would like to include herself. I'd put money she's got something to do with the deaths of Charlotte and Delozier, even if she didn't kill them herself."

Freeze's jaw dropped slowly. "Did some of that chloroform escape and addle your brain on the way over? I'm not going to stick my neck out on something that flimsy."

"I don't expect you to."

"Give me one good reason why she would resort to murder."

"I can't. But there may be a witness who saw her and Delozier together and saw Judith give him money."

"Who?"

"I said 'may be.' I'm not sure."

"If you are withholding information—"

"Yeah, yeah. I thought it might be polite to verify that the witness exists rather than send you off on a wild goose chase."

Freeze lit a cigarette. He glowered. He had practice. "In other words, this is all some hunch of yours."

"There's that." I pointed to the jar and a small bottle it had contained. "Take that little bit of evidence, and the evidence of her not getting sick to her stomach, and a witness with information that's halfway decent, and pretty soon you've got a wad."

"If there's really a witness."

"If there's really a witness."

***

The afternoon had left me sweaty and cranky. Talking to Freeze had also started me wondering whether I'd been too optimistic about the importance of what Arlene had found. I headed for home to plunge myself into a lukewarm bath and then sit on the back steps.

The sight of Connelly's car parked in front of the house upended those plans. As I went up the short sidewalk to the front door, I heard giggles and voices from the backyard. His kids were with him. Stopping just long enough to splash water on my face in the bathroom, I kicked off my shoes and padded barefoot out the kitchen door.

When I had bought my cozy little cottage not quite a year ago, the old shed in the backyard leaned so precariously its collapse seemed imminent. Somehow it had made it through winter, and judging by the activity now going on around it, it was destined to survive a few more. Mick Connelly, stripped to his undershirt, strained to keep a sturdy upright post in place under the sagging corner. A sheen of sweat covered his shoulders and biceps. Standing on a chest beside him, Seamus pounded a board into place between post and roof. He wore overalls and a shirt that had retired before its owner.

Owen, Connelly's little boy by adoption, trotted over to me from where he'd been trying to lure our cat off the porch to play with a piece of string. "How come your kitty won't come out here and play with me?"

"Because she doesn't like boys," said his sister, who'd left her seat in the grass.

"Nah, it's because she's smart and stays on the porch. She knows it's dangerous for kitties to wander. A mean dog might chase her and bite off her ear." I made a silly face and growled.

With a giggle Owen took off running. Brigid chased after him, barking. Work on the shed had halted at least temporarily. Connelly walked toward me, catching his breath.

"You two stay out of there until we get it braced up better," he said to the kids. "Take Uncle Seamus a jar of water. He's been working hard."

The kids filled a Mason jar from a pail on the porch and went running to where Seamus rested astride a sawhorse. He was slipping one hand through his wavy silver hair to cool his head. Connelly lowered himself to the stoop and stretched his legs. "Feels good to sit down."

The sight of him in an undershirt brought to mind the few nights we'd been a couple.

"Beer?" I made to get up.

"I'll stick with water, thanks. I want to get a bit more done on that shed before we take off. Otherwise, the whole thing's likely to fall down on someone."

"I tried to convince Seamus we should tear it down."

"Don't want to do that. Where would you store tools? Get that post in and boards replaced here and there, and it will be right as rain."

"Where did you get a new piece of lumber like that? Oh…"

Connelly grinned. "Yeah. Your friend Rachel. Where did you think that stack of new boards in there came from?"

"Outside is Seamus's territory," I said primly.

"So is the kitchen." His eyes twinkled.

Brigid came up to join us before I could answer. Owen was leaning on the sawhorse talking to Seamus.

"Did you tell her about ice cream?" Bridget asked with a secretive look at her father.

Connelly looped an arm around her. "Just getting ready to, Robin Redbreast." He turned to me. "Miss Brigid here is having a birthday party, and I've been told, under threat of having my nose pulled off, to ask you if you would attend."

"There's going to be ice cream," the little girl said, still giggling at the idea of noses being pulled off. "And cake, too!"

"That's right, my friend Thompson's wife volunteered to bake a cake."

"And ice it in blue."

"Is that your favorite color?"

Brigid's pigtails danced as she nodded.

I'd never had a birthday party. I'd been to several for my childhood friend Wee Willie Ryan, though. He'd been killed in action almost a year ago, and memories of him still brought a wave of sadness. Brigid's excitement outshone it.

"I would love to come. How old are you going to be?"

"Ten."

Maybe some pretty barrettes or hair ribbons, I

thought. Or a diary, since she didn't have a mother to talk to.

"She had her eye on a little microscope she saw at Rike's, of all things."

"But Dad said policemen don't make that kind of money, not even sergeants. But that's okay. Just the party is grand, and I'll probably get new socks or a blouse or something."

"Or who knows, maybe a magnifying glass. They do the same thing, Robin."

Bridget drew back with a skeptical look. "Dad, you know they don't. A magnifying glass is for looking at bugs and blades of grass and that. It's no good for comparing fibers and fingerprints and looking at blood."

Connelly's mouth opened several seconds before he spoke. I hugged myself to mute my laughter.

"How do you know a microscope's used for things like that?"

"One of the men who uses them down at the station let us come in and see what he does. He let us look through and everything."

"When?"

"When we were waiting out in the hall while you went to see someone in a different office. Hey! What's Uncle Seamus showing Owen?" She raced off.

"Have a hard time keeping up with her?" I asked between chuckles.

"You don't know the half of it." Connelly got to his feet. "I'd better help Seamus get that bracing done so I can get those two home and fed and doing their homework."

"I forgot to ask, did you decide about getting the house?"

He nodded. "We sign the paperwork day after tomorrow. Oh, and Brigid's party won't be for several weeks yet. I'll let you know the date soon as I know my schedule."

Leaning back on my elbows, I watched him join the others. The sound of their voices teasing and blending brought a smile to my face. I'd take this small back stoop over the Barretts' terrace with its chairs, umbrellas and pots overflowing with colorful flowers any day, even though it seemed increasingly likely there were people who'd kill to live like the Barretts.

CHAPTER THIRTY-THREE

"Do you have those photographs rounded up?"

"I do, but I'm not sure I ought to be giving them to you."

It was half past eight the following morning. At the other end of the phone, Kaye's voice sounded uncharacteristically reticent.

"You should unless you're trying to protect someone," I said.

"Of course not! I just don't feel… they're family photographs after all. They're—they're private."

"I don't think Mrs. Barrett would like the idea of your not cooperating, do you? I'll be there in fifteen minutes. If you like, I can just pull up to the kitchen door. I don't need to come in."

"Yes. All right. I'll be waiting."

My car was parked where I often left it, in the gravel lot two blocks from my office. All the way there, I puzzled over Kaye's reluctance. Surely she was too young to be the woman who had sat with Delozier at the Little Red Tavern. She was usually friendly as a puppy. I slid beneath the wheel of my DeSoto and sighed. Maybe I was too suspicious. Maybe the reason was exactly the one she'd given.

The secretary was waiting for me, a manila envelope hugged to her chest. She even managed a smile as she greeted me.

"I hope these are what you needed," she said as she handed it over. "These are good people, the ones in the pictures. I feel like a traitor, knowing I could be getting one of them in trouble."

"But you don't. I wouldn't tell you what I wanted them for, remember?"

Without response, she turned and went up the steps to the house.

It was still hours shy of when the owners of the Little Red Tavern might be expected to show up to clean and ready their pub for opening. I took my empty coffee mug to the postage-stamp-size coffee shop across from my office and brought a full one back to sip at my desk while I looked at the photographs. All the females connected with the Barrett household who matched the description of the older woman who'd sat with Delozier were there. Lola, Nurse Willington, and Judith. My money started out on a candidate I favored over the others, but as I sifted through what I'd learned about each, I realized any one of them could have the motive and the opportunity to make them a killer.

There were two of the photographs, eight by tens

from someone's birthday party, which led me to think briefly of Brigid Connelly. Her homemade cake would be a far cry from the elaborately decorated creation I saw now. It sat at the center of a table in the living room, its position giving no clue whose special day was being recognized.

I studied the faces around it. Lola was in both of the photographs, the force of her smile giving her a sparkle which I hadn't noticed before. Nurse Wellington appeared in one picture only. She stood near Helen, her expression closed. Judith also appeared in both photos. Her hands were clasped decorously in front of her and she wore a bangle bracelet similar to those which Tinker favored. Kaye, whom I didn't consider a suspect but was on my mind because of her odd wariness that morning, hovered at the edges looking awkward as ever and thrilled to be present.

I strained to find some clarity, some insight in the pictures before me. Helen's health was deteriorating. Judith. Lola. The nurse. Any one of them might believe that with Helen out of the way they stood a chance of capturing Simon Barrett's affections. Was one of them willing to hasten Helen's demise? Willing enough to meet Jimmy Delozier and give him money? And did any of it get me any closer to learning who had killed Charlotte?

Raking my hands through my hair, I tossed the combs I'd loosened onto my desk in frustration.

Charlotte had suggested that Helen's reversal in terms of energy might be owing to some mixup in her prescription. Was that really based on something she'd read in a book or seen in a movie? Or, as I theorized, had she witnessed someone tampering with one of Helen's prescription bottles? Someone she was afraid to accuse – or reluctant to – outright.

***

At half past ten there was still no sign of activity at the Little Red Tavern. Ten minutes later when I drove by again, a battered old wreck of a car was pulled up in the farthest corner of its tiny parking strip. Even though the place wouldn't open for more than an hour, I left my DeSoto on the street in case a supply truck wanted to pull in close to the door.

"You back?" the owner said with a frown as I made my appearance through the storage and utility space which I had guessed would offer the only unlocked door.

"Don't worry, it's your missus I want to see."

She grinned and made a show of fluffing nonexistent curls. Then she came to the end of the bar, squeezing past her husband.

I brandished my envelope. "I brought you more photographs. See if you recognize any of these women."

Her husband nudged in and she pretended to elbow him.

"Looks like those people have some mighty nice parties," she said. "That one. That one there's the one who was sitting with Jimmy Delozier."

Her blunt finger stabbed down twice. On Judith Todd.

For the first time, I became aware of a mantle clock on a shelf behind the bar. Its ticking filled the empty room.

"You're sure?"

"Yep. I remembered something else about her after you were in here last time. Just a little bit above her ankle…" Her features puckered in thought. "Her right ankle, inside of it, she had a birthmark. Looked just like a turtle."

CHAPTER THIRTY-FOUR

My hands gripped the steering wheel loosely and precisely. If I let tension claim them, I would be more likely to speed. I would grip so hard I pulled myself forward, straining to get to my destination, and unconsciously pushing harder on the gas. By holding the car to a disciplined pace, I hoped to do the same with my thoughts.

That part didn't work. Although the DeSoto moved down Main Street without creating so much as a ripple in the traffic flow, my brain exceeded the speed limit. I needed to see whether Judith had a birthmark on her ankle. If she did, that would satisfy Freeze's insistence on evidence and he could step in. I still couldn't fathom a woman becoming so obsessed with climbing the social ladder that she would kill two people and plot the death of a third to do it.

Could I be overlooking her real motivation? She was secretary to the man in charge of a secret government project, one important enough that it caused his assistant to chew his fingernails to the quick, one important enough to bring people from

Washington here to meet with him privately. Could Judith be passing information to the enemy? It made the murder-for-marriage scenario look believable in comparison.

Ahead of me I saw the entrance to the Barrett mansion and the pull off at the bottom of the drive which made it so easy for someone to slip away somewhere late at night in the car left down there. With effort I slowed my speed even more and rolled up the driveway. Above the wall of the raised terrace I could see a head in one of the lounge chairs. Tinker probably. I went to the front door.

"Ms. Sullivan." Griggs nodded acknowledgment as he admitted me.

"Good morning, Griggs. If Miss Todd can spare a moment I need to speak to her."

"Miss Todd?" My request startled him. It was always a family member or the stalwart Kaye that I'd asked for on my past visits. "Yes, I'll—"

"Judith's not here, I'm afraid." Simon Barrett, appearing from the vicinity of his office, had overheard. "We've nothing to do this morning. We're waiting on some visitors who'll be arriving this afternoon. She and Arlene went down to Rike's to pick up some things that Helen asked for."

"I did no such thing." The sound of Helen's voice, downstairs and at that time of day, was so unexpected all three of us turned.

"Helen!"

Her husband stood frozen in place. His face radiated equal parts shock and joy. Helen propelled herself slowly toward us in her wheelchair. She'd come down the hall that led to the elevator, and she'd come alone. Nurse Wellington and a beaming Lola came down the front stairs, Kaye behind them.

"Darling! Darling!" Simon rushed toward her and planted a kiss on her cheek. His raised voice drew Jack from his office. A smile broke over his face. Hooking his cane on his wrist, he applauded.

"Lola's been helping me practice going up and down my sitting room while everyone thought I was napping – which I still do far too often. Nurse Wellington caught us today and gave me a terrible scolding, so I thought I'd better come clean."

"No wonder she didn't have any energy some days," the nurse muttered.

"I'm hoping I'll last long enough to greet your guests from Washington. Now what's this about my asking for something from Rike's? I didn't."

"Perhaps I misunderstood." Simon brushed it aside.

I hated to spoil Helen's triumph and the joy those who loved her were feeling, but a coldness had filled me. Arlene was with Judith. Arlene hated Judith.

"I hate to interrupt," I cut in, "but this is important. Can anyone tell me if Judith has a birthmark?"

The Barretts had forgotten my presence. Even

Jack's face showed annoyance at my intrusion. It was Kaye who spoke.

"She does, yes. On the inside of her leg." She indicated her right ankle. "But you only notice it if she crosses her legs, and it's not very large." Her shoulders hunched as she gave her embarrassed giggle. "It looks like a gumdrop."

"What's so important about a tattoo?" Simon snapped.

"A witness saw her with Jimmy Delozier. Giving him money. Only days before Charlotte was killed. The witness even described the tattoo."

Jack's indrawn breath told me he'd grasped the significance.

"That and other things have convinced me she hired Delozier to kill Charlotte and then killed him so he wouldn't talk."

"What? That's prepos—" Simon broke off as his assistant McDowell burst in.

"Did you take one of the samples, Simon? Did you send one downtown?"

"No, why?" His attention shifted. He tensed. "What's wrong?"

McDowell rubbed a hand across his mouth. "The safe was ajar. The door. I looked. One's missing."

"Did you lock…?"

"Yes."

"Where's Noah?"

"On the terrace with Tinker," Kaye said.

Griggs sprang to fetch him.

"I don't suppose Judith is back there?" Simon's voice was tight.

"No, sir. I thought she said something to you about going shopping. Since you'd told us to take the morning off to relax."

"God in heaven!" Helen breathed. "What Miss Sullivan told us about Judith killing… She's got our daughter, Simon! You have to call the police!"

His thatch of white hair was already shaking.

"You don't understand. That vial she took contains a chemical weapon the Nazis have been developing. If exposed to air, the mixture creates a nerve gas that kills in seconds. It only contains a small amount, but…"

Swallowing a cry, Helen sagged back in her chair. Nurse Wellington rushed to her side. Helen motioned her back.

Simon Barrett, captain of industry, a man who could snap his fingers and make bankers and men of influence jump, turned to me.

"I'm too close to this. Help me. What do I do?"

I was wondering the same thing.

"We have to assume she really is headed to Rike's," I said slowly. "She mentioned it. She probably knows we'll come looking for her as soon as you realize the sample is missing. Maybe she wants us to follow her there."

"But why?"

"Because she's mad," Jack said. "Arlene believed she had designs on you – that she expected Mother to die and that you'd marry her."

"She was helping things along,' I said. "She switched one of Helen's medicines."

Nurse Wellington, understanding instantly, gasped. Noah ran in from the terrace with Tinker beside him.

"Dad! Is it true? About Judith?"

His father nodded.

"The police, Simon, please!" Helen begged.

"No, from what he's said about the contents of that vial he's right. There's too much chance that they'd rush her, in which case she might drop it."

Deliberately or because she panicked. She'd kill innocent people. Including their daughter.

My thoughts revised themselves. She intended to release the vial's poisonous contents no matter what. There was no way back for her now. She couldn't return to her job. The theft of the vial from the safe alone was enough to send her to jail. Her guilt in two murders would likely get her the electric chair.

"She's gone to Rike's because it will be full of shoppers for… whatever she means to do." I was thinking aloud. "She may see it as evening scores, somehow. I think Jack's right that there's an element of madness in the fantasy she created."

I turned to Simon. "I worked at Rike's for six years,

some of them in loss prevention. I know every inch of the store. I probably can't sneak up on her, and trying to disarm her would be too risky. I'll try to lure her to an area where any damage she tries with that concoction she's carrying will be minimal, and where I can get her away from Arlene."

"Let's go."

"She's probably planned how to handle you. She won't know what to try with me. You stay and get on the phone to Chief Wurstner himself. Explain the danger and tell his men to wait outside – at the ends of the Ludlow Street alley and as far as possible from the other service entrances."

"Jack, you're the levelheaded one in the family. Do as she says." Simon gestured at me to start moving. "I won't come inside, but it will save time if I drive and drop you off so you don't have to park."

I saw the logic, and nodded.

"What about the people from Washington? They'll be landing in less than two hours," Noah burst out.

"You'll have to fill in for me. Explain what's happened. Smooth feathers if you can, and if you can't, you can't. John—" pointing at McDowell, he snapped out more orders "—you do the technical briefing. You'd do the bulk of it anyway. And John – don't apologize. We knew odds of success on this were long when we started. They knew it too. We gave it our best shot. Perhaps what we've learned in the course of our experiments will prove useful in some way."

I turned to Jack. "As soon as you've called the police, call Abner Simms. He's head of Rike's security." I rattled off the number and extension. Kaye scribbled them on a pad she'd produced. "Tell him not to create a panic, and to expect a call from me from millinery or the employee lounge on Three. Tell him to alert anybody in the store who worked with me and have them keep an eye out in case I have a message to pass."

"Bring our daughter home, Simon." Helen's voice wavered.

Her husband seized her hand and kissed it fiercely. "I will, love. I promise."

CHAPTER THIRTY-FIVE

"I lied to my wife." Simon Barrett gripped the wheel of my DeSoto with grim determination. He hadn't argued when I told him it was just outside the side door and tossed him my keys.

"When you promised to bring Arlene back safely?"

He nodded. "If there was any chance – any chance – I could reason with Judith, or get close enough to get between her and Arlene, I'd leave this car in the middle of the street and run inside when we get there."

"It might make things worse if she saw you."

"Yes. And while the sample in that vial might only kill a handful of people, it might just as easily kill dozens. We've seen what it does to guinea pigs, but we don't know how many human lives an amount like that would claim. We don't experiment on people in this country, thank God."

"And you've been cooking this up in your back room?" I asked with more control than I felt.

"What do you take us for, Miss Sullivan? We've been trying to develop an antidote, something that would neutralize this... well, we call it Hellwater. Our best bet was a coating for Allied gas masks, but our best bet hasn't worked so far, and I doubt it will. Any actual experimentation we do is at our main laboratory downtown. It's larger. It has an airtight chamber."

We were passing the fairgrounds now. A truck pulled out in front of us. Simon swore and continued.

"It's the antidote itself we've been working on in the lab at the house. The War Department thinks if the tide turns against the Nazis, which it already has, they may use this nerve agent on Allied troops. On their initial visit they suggested we keep the samples in the safe at the house because they thought it was safer than downtown, with fewer people around."

"But Judith knew the combination."

"No, but she was often there when I opened it. I'd be giving her directions on something to do when John McDowell and I were heading downtown. She could easily have noted the numbers I dialed. Judith is a very smart woman."

We were at the edge of downtown. I spoke quickly. "In case I'm not around when this ends, there are things you need to know. Evidence, in case Judith survives." As I talked, I pulled the envelope of photographs from my purse and dropped them on the seat between us. "Jimmy Delozier used to drink at a place called the Little Red Tavern. One of the owners picked Judith out in these photographs as a woman who met him there and gave him a packet of money. She's the one who told me about the birthmark on Judith's leg."

I sketched in how Charlotte had suggested to Nurse Wellington that the bout of declining health Helen was experiencing might be from a pharmacy error in her prescription, but how in her last, frightened phone call, she'd told Mrs. Salmon that she'd seen something and needed to get someplace safe.

"My God. Judith was trying to poison my wife."

"Yes, I think so."

Rike's was only a block ahead now. I squeezed in one more thing. "Tell the police to stay out of sight. I'm going to try to get Judith out into the alley to the north. It's called Booher Lane." Otherwise, there was too much chance she would unleash the poison she carried in a store full of people.

Simon stopped the car in the middle of Main Street. I jumped out, waited for break in traffic, and dashed across.

***

The faint, familiar smell of Rike's slid around me like a friend's arm over my shoulders. Its undefinable blend of wooden floors, scent from the perfume counter, polish, and new clothes steadied me. A stoop-shouldered floor walker who stood six-foot-two in spite of the stoop appeared to be straightening stacks of shirts in a side aisle. His name was Gibbons, and he'd been working at Rike's when I started there part time as a high school kid. He came toward me.

"Need help?" he murmured.

"Tell Abner to keep the house phone in the lounge on Three open for me. Have the girls on Two and Three get a few rolling garment racks with an armful of items on them close to the main aisles."

He gave a shallow bow as if he'd offered help and I'd declined. If Judith and her hostage were on the mezzanine and happened to notice the interaction, it wouldn't arouse suspicion. Unless they were directly above me, Judith wasn't likely to recognize me at that distance since she wasn't expecting me.

From my vantage point I could see almost nothing of people on the mezzanine except for a few whose steps from time to time wove closer to the inner railing. Struggling to move no more quickly than a hurried shopper, I made a circuit through the street level. At the back of my mind, the familiar registered: the barrel for collecting worn out silk stockings; the long cosmetics counter; the millinery section where I'd drooled over hats. The front of my mind was alert for something unusual, odd movements, a disturbance.

I went up the stairs to the mezzanine. A mother

with an eager little boy beside her stood at the candy counter. Two women chattered as they placed orders for baked goods while an older couple waited behind them. I moved to the railing to scan the crowd below me, when instead I spotted my quarry here on the same level I was. Directly across from me.

Judith was wearing a suit of robin's egg blue, brighter than her usual plumage. Something special for the Washington visitors, perhaps. She had one arm around Arlene as if they were best chums. How had she persuaded Arlene to accompany her when Arlene detested her? Did the girl know about the deadly little vial Judith was carrying? Even if she did, why hadn't she jumped out of the car and escaped? Arlene was no coward. She would have risked injury, maybe even death, rather than become Judith's victim. What was Judith holding over her?

The secretary saw me. She turned the girl beside her and the two of them strolled toward the staircase leading up. I followed. I needed to get Arlene away from her captor on the floor they were headed for, or on the one above that. Those two floors were devoted to women's apparel. There were rows of garments Arlene could duck behind if I could momentarily separate her from Judith. They were also the floors with which Arlene would be most familiar. She could make a beeline a few floors down to an exit.

From the fourth floor on up, clothing gave way to household furnishings: housewares and china, mattresses and linens. Then to sewing machines, sporting equipment, toys. I could lose Judith on any of those floors and in practically any department if I chose. The plan I had in mind, however, the only one I could think of to save unwary shoppers from a horrible death, called for other tactics.

CHAPTER THIRTY-SIX

At the top of stairs, Judith spun and peered past me. A beat of hesitation and she headed toward Better Sportswear. Arlene threw a look in my direction, then went along meekly at some word from Judith.

Fearful that I'd lose sight of them, I murmured apologies to a formidably corseted matron as I squeezed around her and took the stairs two at a time. When I reached the second floor, the pair I was following appeared to be looking at sweaters. I knew by the tilt of Judith's head that she was watching for me.

I sauntered. My heart was punching my chest so hard and rapidly I could scarcely breathe. It was impossible to see whether Judith had the vial of chemicals in her hand or not. If she did, I couldn't risk tackling her or slugging her in the jaw. She might drop the vial and spill its contents as she fell back. Neither could I use the gun in the holster at the small of my back. Not in a place like this, with people bobbing and veering and changing direction all around.

Did Judith have a plan? She wasn't attempting to give me the slip. She was standing her ground. As she watched my approach, her gaze kept flicking over my shoulder. Six feet away from her, I stopped to assess.

"Who's with you?" she asked.

Ah-hah. She hadn't expected me to turn up. She'd expected... who? Simon. It had to be Simon.

"No one. I'm all by my lonesome," I said.

"You're lying."

"Go away. Please." Arlene was as white as funeral flowers. "She's given Mother something. Something she's swallowed. She said if I came here with her and did what she said, she'd call and tell Nurse Wellington the antidote."

"Your mother's perfectly fine. I just saw her. If you're expecting Simon, Judith, don't hold your breath. He has muckety-mucks coming in from Washington, remember?"

"He'll come all right, to save his precious daughter."

Judith dipped her free hand into her pocket and brought out a bottle as small as the ones that held pricey perfume at the counter downstairs. She rocked it gently.

My stomach clenched. "That's an inert sample, Judith. A dud. John McDowell took the real ones downtown. Simon has suspected for several days that you were up to something."

"He couldn't have."

"Why? Because you thought having Charlotte killed would keep anyone else from learning you'd replaced Helen's heart pills with low-dosage ones?"

"She couldn't be sure what she saw, though. Just that I was in Helen's bathroom when they were away at a doctor's appointment. I didn't see her, just heard the door click. But why take chances?"

Judith's eyes glowed with triumph – and madness.

"That houseman they'd fired would have done the job at half the price to even scores. I knew the time of day she walked. I knew the route. I left a few flourishes in her room so she'd be too rattled to notice a car coming toward her."

Judith waggled the vial.

"This isn't a dud. I'm going to loosen the cap and drop it into your pocket and give you a nice, hard shove, Arlene dear." She thumbed the cap of the bottle. "When the contents spill, they'll kill you and everyone around you. I'll be too far away. I'll be forced to tell the truth – how I saw you take the sample and tried to stop you—"

"That's a lie!"

"How you've always been unstable, but your parents couldn't see it."

"Maggie, is what she said... the stuff in the bottle...?"

"Yes."

Arlene made a mewing sound.

A clerk approached, pleasant and white-haired. Not one I recognized.

"May I help you?"

The vial Judith held was hidden in the fold of her skirt now.

"Just friends who haven't seen each other in a while catching up." I manufactured a laugh. "Thank you, though. Lovely sweaters. We'll find you if we're tempted."

With a smile and a nod the clerk turned away. I thought how attractive Judith was. In her pretty suit and feathered hat, she fitted into the scene as unremarkably as any other well-dressed woman shopping here. Then she brought the vial back into view.

With the arm she had around Arlene's shoulders, she pulled the girl closer against her. She was trying to force the breast pocket of Arlene's suit to pouch outward so she could complete her plan, but the fabric wasn't cooperating. I had to act fast.

"If Arlene gets away, no one's going to believe her accusations if you tell that cockamamie story you've concocted," I said. "But if I get away..." I patted my shoulder bag. "I have evidence linking you to Delozier's murder, if not Charlotte's as well. The cops know me. They'll believe me about you having that poison. You can't stop us both. Which one will it be?"

"I'll kill myself and her along with me!" Judith brandished the vial.

"No you won't." My heart thudded. "You might if Simon had come, to punish him by making him watch his daughter die."

"All I've done for him – for them – and when I offered to start planning a party to celebrate when the war ends, he said his wife would take care of that! He told me to take the morning off and waved his hand like he was shooing away a-a fly!"

Innocent comments by a man with too much on his mind, but it had pushed her over the edge.

"Arlene or me? Which one of us do you need out of the way, Judith?"

As we talked, I'd been drifting backward. Judith followed, her plans crumbling around her, yet determined not to let me escape. One more step put her in range of the sparsely filled clothing rack a stockgirl had just dragged into a side aisle. The garments on it hid my hand as I caught the rack's metal upright at waist level and, aided by shoulder and hip, shoved it at Judith. I didn't bump her hard enough to make her drop her lethal cargo, just hard enough to distract her and cause her to stagger a step.

Arlene seized the opportunity. Rather than struggle to pull away, the quick-thinking girl dropped down out of Judith's encircling arm and turned a backward somersault. Like some fleet-footed African animal, she sprinted off the opposite way, leaping over a little boy who had stooped to pull up his sock.

Judith spared but a second's glance for her lost captive. That was enough for me to dodge around the rack I'd shoved. In an aisle parallel to Judith's, I headed in the general direction of the Ladies Lounge, moving as quickly as I could without drawing attention from shoppers. Judith followed, trying to close the gap between us but smart enough to keep her speed in check too.

As I slipped through the aisles I zigzagged once. I used small stand mirrors adorning some counters to check the progress of my pursuer. Just ahead on my right was a long table filled with markdown goods. It had stood in the same spot since I worked at Rike's. Unlike the actual counters around it, it had no bottom. Grabbing hold of the edge I swung under it and out the other side, a move I'd seen a young shoplifter execute in my floorwalker days.

Once again I was one aisle over from Judith. When she turned to move into the same aisle, she found her way blocked by one of the large and elegant white columns spaced throughout the store. By the time she got to a place where she could cut over, I had gained another smidgen of precious time. I waved to her from the Up staircase.

I was taking a chance luring her through this store filled with people, but simply going down and out any exit but the one I'd chosen carried just as great a risk with people passing on the sidewalks. She'd been single-minded in her pursuit of Simon Barrett. I was gambling that she would be equally single-minded in her pursuit of me; that she not only wanted to silence me, but now burned to destroy me.

As soon as I reached the floor where women with ration coupons and plenty of money could buy better dresses and evening wear, I sprinted for a corner and a nondescript door marked *Employees*. The smell of dill pickle greeted me as I stepped through. Half a dozen women sat at the table eating an early lunch. A mix of curious and wary faces turned to look at me. At the house phone a young woman punched in numbers and held the receiver out to me.

"Don't worry, dear. If anyone comes snooping around, I'll shoo them away." A motherly little woman with a pencil behind her ear picked up a clipboard and squeezed out the way I'd come.

"Ab—" I said into the phone.

"Exit 8. Got it. What—?"

"Spread some of those quilted covers they use to deliver furniture outside the door so the glass bottle she has doesn't break if she drops it." If she threw it deliberately, in an alley with brick walls on both sides, all bets were off. "Get any delivery people who might be out there out of the way. You stay back too. Out of sight."

"But—"

"If you hear a shot, wait at least five minutes or until I give you the all clear. If another woman comes out, black hair, detain her."

The only way Judith was going to walk out without me was if she unleashed the devil's brew she carried.

CHAPTER THIRTY-SEVEN

"Empty cartons," I ordered as I hung up.

The same girl who had handed me the phone sprang to a stack of cardboard boxes in one corner before my eyes had settled on them. She dumped the contents of the top one and thrust it into my arms. It had tape covering holes here and there and was battered from repeated uses due to wartime shortages. I boosted it up to hide my face.

"Ask the woman who went out, the one with the clipboard, ask her if there's anyone else around. If there's not, open the door for me."

I stepped back as she departed. A moment later the door swung wide.

"All clear."

Using the box as cover, I scanned the store for faces as I moved. I spotted Judith looking around uncertainly. She came in my direction without seeing me. I moved along the perimeter out of the way of shoppers like a good little stock clerk. When Judith dodged into a dressing room to see if I'd gone to ground there, I ditched the carton I'd been carrying and made for the stairs again. It took a moment before she noticed me and followed. Going up wasn't logical. She was likely to realize that, but I had to buy Abner time. Furniture was several floors above us, but the big quilted pads for delivering new furniture to customers wouldn't be up there, surely. They'd be down where purchases were loaded into vans. Wouldn't they?

I made my stand in the china department, amidst displays of Spode, Royal Dalton and American made Lenox. There weren't as many customers here as there were in clothing.

"May I help you?" the clerk inquired as I turned to watch Judith's approach.

"You can stay away and keep any customers away without being obvious." I kept my voice low. "There's a situation. Abner Simms knows about it."

She stared for a moment, frozen. Then, with one hand clutching the lapel of her suit as if to hold herself upright, she turned and left. Her elbow brushed against Judith's as they passed.

When Judith got within six feet of me, I edged sideways, around two tables shoved together for a double-wide display of lunch and dinner linens.

"I could have given you the slip downstairs, Judith. I came up here so you could see that. I want to offer you a deal."

"You want money?" The corners of her mouth

curled in a sneer. "How predictable. A grubby little detective who probably doesn't have two cents in her bank account trying to blackmail me. Do you think I'm stupid enough to give you a nickel for whatever proof against me you claim to have in your purse? When you're sticking your nose into that doxie's death ruined everything for me? I could have been Simon Barrett's wife! I could have had prestige, social position—"

"Did I say anything about money?" I asked sharply.

She'd been following me around the table, trying to close the distance between us while I inched away. We circled the pretty linens in a deadly game of musical chairs.

"Let's try this," I said. "You set that little bottle down very carefully between those stacks of napkins in front of you. I set the evidence in my purse down over here—"

"Evidence which doesn't exist, or which you've given copies of to the police."

"Maybe, maybe not."

"All I have to do is explain it away – which I can, once I get rid of you. If other people get killed, well, that's tragic. I tried to prevent it, tried to get you to give me the sample after you snatched it from Arlene."

I'd stalled her as long as I dared. Her whole focus now was on killing me, but to do that she had to make sure she was close enough for the poison to reach me. If she grew impatient she might miscalculate, or act in frustration. The only way to save the lives of innocent shoppers, and maybe my own as well, was to decoy her out of the store.

Turning, I swerved past the end of a table of pitchers and trays, and into a main aisle. It was just about where I'd planned to be when our ring-around-the-rosie at the linen table ended. Meanwhile, Judith was now at the far corner where I'd originally stood. She'd be slower to thread her way out after me.

When I estimated she would have reached the main aisle, I glanced over my shoulder only to find her closer than expected. As I looked away, she broke into a trot. I did likewise.

How close did the unleashed poison have to be to me to be effective? Something Simon Barrett had said made me think roughly six feet. I wasn't sure, but that was all I had to go on.

At the Down staircase I took the steps two at a time, eliciting a couple of warnings. There were no helpful mirrors here. When I reached the third floor and the stairs doubled back to go down again, I saw Judith across from me. She was gaining.

I took off running in a tight circle that brought me directly behind where she'd be when she came off the stairs. The towering stairwell and one of the big white columns hid me momentarily. Long enough for me to spot a service counter, slide behind it, and crouch at the feet of a startled clerk who was manning the cash register.

"I'm helping Abner Simms," I said, a finger to my lips to implore her secrecy. "A woman in a blue hat with black and green feathers – do you see her?"

She scanned the store nervously. "Yes. In Better Dresses."

I had to make sure Judith saw me and continued the chase so that she didn't randomly unleash the poison in a fit of frustration – but I had to control the chase too.

"Is she looking this way?"

"No, but a customer's heading over to be rung up..."

I bolted from my hiding place. When I was several yards away, I stopped and waited for Judith, whose head was whirling back and forth, to spot me. Pretending to notice her at the same instant, I ran for the stairs again.

Behind me, I heard Judith yell about shoplifting. There were exclamations as I passed. An arm swung out to detain me. I spun it up out of the way. I was on Two now. One more flight of stairs to go. I couldn't risk having Judith above me or abreast of me on the zig-zag stairs. Halfway down the final flight, I gripped the bannister and vaulted onto the ground floor.

My goal was in sight now, a nondescript door in the wall behind the Notions department. Beyond it lay a storeroom, and, at the back of it, opening onto an alley named Booher Lane, a door marked with the numeral 8.

Gibbons, the tall, stooped floor walker who'd met me when I first entered the store, now held a pencil and clipboard and appeared to be checking items on a table holding spools of thread, spare hosiery clips, bobby pins, and sundry other notions items well removed from the door to the stockroom. His head remained bent, but his eyebrows raised in question.

"Let me know when you see a brunette in a bright blue hat – when she sees me. Keep everyone else out."

Moistening two fingers he flipped back the top sheet on his clipboard. "Now."

With a great gulp of air, I looked around me and slipped through the door to the storeroom. It was much as I remembered. Several naked mannequins. Three disembodied arms stowed on a shelf. A line of heads on another shelf, waiting until they were needed. A dolly and a wooden pushcart were shoved against one wall. But cartons and crates, most stacked chest high and occasionally taller, occupied most of the space.

I ran to the door leading out to the alley and gave it a hard shove. The glimpse I got showed everything clear to the right. On the other side I had to trust Abner had done as I asked. Freeing my Smith & Wesson from its holster, I crouched between two rows of cartons just as Judith burst in from the store.

Her head whipped left and right hunting me. Her arm was outstretched. I couldn't see the tiny vial suspended from her fingertips, but I knew it was there. As I had hoped, the closing alley door drew her attention. She bounded toward it with the fleetness of a pouncing cat. One hard shove and she was out. She staggered but recovered her footing an instant before my bullet shattered her shoulder.

Knocked to her knees by the impact, she fell onto to her belly with arms outstretched. As she landed, I saw a shaft of silver smash down on her left forearm. Judith shrieked. The nasty little vial she'd carried rolled uncomfortably close to the edge of two mattresses shoved against each other outside the door.

Judith's left hand was in spasm. Her right hand clawed weakly at the mattress beneath her. Lest her thrashing increase and jostle the vial off onto the hard surface of the alley, I straddled her and rested the nose of my .38 against the back of her head and told her to lie still.

My temples were drenched with sweat. I wondered how long they'd been that way. I became aware of city sounds, lovely sounds, sounds of life that meant I was alive too. To my left Abner Simms stood bent over, gulping in an effort not to lose his breakfast and gripping a golf club. A few more gulps and he spoke.

"No time to get furniture wraps. Dropped the mattresses off the fire escape and dragged them over."

"I thought I told you to stay away," I managed.

Still upside down, he tilted his face toward me. "My store, my responsibility."

I understood.

CHAPTER THIRTY-EIGHT

A week later Abner and I had lunch on an upper floor of the department store where we had fought so frantically to save unsuspecting lives. We weren't in one of the dining rooms, we were in his office. A small table had been set up complete with white linen and napkins folded in fans. We were sipping whiskey which Abner had offered and which we both preferred to the champagne waiting to be opened in a stand beside the table.

"That's some golf swing you have," I said, ending awkward silence as we avoided mentioning those heart stopping moments in the alley. "You must be the devil to beat when you play."

The nightmare acknowledged, he chuckled. Then he frowned. "You do know you never smash a club straight down like that, don't you?"

I gave way to gale after gale of laughter. Relief. Release. "I kind of figured you didn't."

His expression was sheepish now. "You hadn't come out, and it was the only backup plan I had, knocking her on the head. In that split second when I heard your shot, I couldn't stop. Best I could do was pull back."

And a good thing he had, I thought. A blow to her head with the kind of force he'd used would have killed her. I hoped he never realized that.

He eyed the champagne. "You like that stuff?"

"Not much."

"The management wanted to pull out all the stops to thank you. You better take it with you when you leave."

"How about sharing it with the clerks who helped when we needed it?"

"Now there's a thought."

He went to his intercom and reeled off a handful of names to his secretary, along with instructions for them to come to his office half an hour before quitting time. "Better tell them it's a little celebration so they don't worry. Get some finger sandwiches and fancy cookies from food service."

"You might add Gibbons the floorwalker to the roster," I suggested.

"Oh, yeah. He can be the thorn among the roses."

He finished with his secretary just in time to admit a waitress wheeling in a cart of silver domed dishes. I raised my eyebrows when she served up slices of beef tenderloin with baby vegetables.

Abner chuckled. "It's not something new in one of the restaurants. They cooked it up special for us."

"Here's to being around to enjoy it." I raised my glass.

Abner returned the gesture. "I don't think I'll ever get over seeing those fire department fellows coming in from both ends of the alley looking like spacemen in their masks and outfits. How's the girl?"

"Arlene? She's okay." It helped that she now knew her mother's recent bouts of exhaustion had resulted from Helen pushing herself to exercise in order to build up strength.

"I overheard Barrett telling the cops that he and his people were trying to concoct an antidote to that stuff in the bottle. Is that true?"

"Them and groups at two other companies. None of them have succeeded so far."

That information came to me from Kaye, who had been pressed into service as Noah's secretary for the visit by the Washington dignitaries. She hadn't said it was secret and I hadn't signed any papers.

The Barretts had been effusive in their thanks to me, but underneath it, all of them except maybe Arlene had been relieved to see the back of me. I reminded them of unpleasantness in their lives. I had poked and pried at things they wanted kept private. Whether Jack was glad I had found the person responsible for Charlotte's death or was merely bolstered by a sense he had done his duty to her was a question I'd never be able to answer. His final check, which included a generous bonus, went a long way toward consoling me.

It was the gratitude of the woman who had started it all, Mrs. Salmon, that made my swim through the sewers of the rich and privileged all worthwhile. She had given me a beautiful cameo brooch, by far the finest piece of jewelry I'd ever owned. She'd hugged me and told me not to be shy if I ever needed a favor.

"You have something on your mind?" Abner asked. "You've gone awfully quiet."

"I saw a hat on the way in. I was wondering whether I should succumb, now that I've practically got money to burn," I lied.

"Well, then, you may be interested in what I've got to say. Before the business last week, I'd been thinking about retirement. Have time for golf. Take some trips with the wife once the world gets up and running again. Standing there in that alley and realizing my life might end in seconds helped me decide."

He took a hefty swallow of whiskey before continuing.

"I'm going to stay in this job one more year. After that, it's yours if you want it. Management agrees. Don't say No right off the way you have whenever I tried to tempt you back to work here. The salary that goes with this job is good. Your employee discount would let you buy every hat in the store. You'd have regular hours. Think about it, Maggie."

I took a minute before I answered. "I appreciate the offer, Ab, and I promise I'll give it some thought. The thing is, I kind of like what I do."

With a sigh he reached under his jacket. "I figured you'd say that. The Rike family said if you did, to give you this."

The amount of the check he handed me made my eyes pop.

"It's their way of thanking you. For putting your life on the line and for preventing this store from being linked to tragedy."

I handed it back to him.

"I can't take this. I was paid by my client. What I did here was part of my job. It was what any decent person would do."

Amusement twitched his mouth to the side.

"I warned them you wouldn't take it. They said if you didn't, to tell you that you have a lifetime employee discount then. Use it or not as you like. They also want you to pick out something nice for yourself – maybe a hat or a set of dishes – on them."

Nudging my empty plate away, I smiled at the good-natured man across from me, a man with whom a few minutes and a small vial of poison had forged a bond which no one but the two of us could ever appreciate.

"I won't say no to the discount. Instead of a gift for me, though, maybe you could arrange a favor. The daughter of a policeman friend fell in love with a microscope you have on display here."

"Okay..." He wasn't following yet.

"The kid has a birthday coming up, but a cop's salary doesn't stretch to a gift that expensive. It might, though, if the microscope got marked down because it was a display model."

Abner's grin turned him into a boy again. "Maybe it has a couple of scratches? Or one corner of the box is dented? I was noticing something like that just today."

— The End —

READ ALL THE MAGGIE SULLIVAN MYSTERIES

No Game for a Dame

When a stranger who threatened her and wrecked her office winds up dead, 1940s private eye Maggie Sullivan finds herself facing a crime boss.

Tough Cookie

A high stakes swindler Maggie is hunting is found floating in the river. Now someone wants to silence her – and the corpse is strangely active.

Don't Dare a Dame

A 25-year-old murder jeopardizes Maggie's future as a private eye as well as her life when it points toward people with political connections.

Shamus in a Skirt

Murder and theft at a posh hotel pits Maggie against well-heeled suspects fleeing the war in Europe.

Maximum Moxie

Kidnapping, murder and a child's plea draw Maggie into a new case days before the attack on Pearl Harbor.

Dames Fight Harder

Maggie becomes the last hope for a friend accused of murder.

Uncivil Defense

To save innocent lives, Maggie must learn who killed a newly released convict during a blackout drill.

Ration of Lies

Grief-stricken over the death of a friend in WWII, Maggie struggles to prove the innocence of a Japanese-American man accused of starting a fatal fire.

ABOUT THE AUTHOR

M. Ruth Myers received a Shamus Award from Private Eye Writers of America for the third book in her Maggie Sullivan mysteries series. She is the author of more than a dozen books in assorted genres, some written under the name Mary Ruth Myers. If you shine a bright light in her eyes, she'll admit to one husband, one daughter, one son-in-law, one grandson and one cat – all of whom she adores. She lives in Ohio.

www.ingramcontent.com/pod-product-compliance
Lightning Source LLC
Chambersburg PA
CBHW020315160726
47992CB00004B/1548